Reply to a Letter from Helga

Reply to a Letter from Helga

Bergsveinn Birgisson

TRANSLATED BY PHILIP ROUGHTON
ILLUSTRATIONS BY KJARTAN HALLUR

amazon crossing 🌐

Text copyright © 2011 by Bergsveinn Birgisson
English translation copyright © 2013 by Philip Roughton
Illustrations copyright © 2010 by Kjartan Hallur

Reply to a Letter from Helga was first published in 2011 by Bjartur as *Svar við bréfi Helgu*. Translated from Icelandic by Philip Roughton. Published in English by AmazonCrossing in 2013.

Published by AmazonCrossing
P.O. Box 400818
Las Vegas, NV 89140

ISBN-13: 9781612187174
ISBN-10: 161218717X
Library of Congress Control Number: 2012913020

It was once a clear morning.

It was many years ago.

The two of them walked along the sidewalk

and held hands facing the rising sun.

Facing the rising sun

both considering their own way.

Now they both walk their own way

and hold hands.

Hold hands

across a clear morning.

—*Stefán Hörður Grímsson, "They"*

1

Kolkustaðir, Feast of the Beheading of St. John the Baptist, 1997

Dear Helga,

Some people die from what is beyond them. Others die because death has been in them for ages, clamping their veins from within. They all die. Each in his own way. Some fall to the floor midsentence. Others depart peacefully in a dream. Do their dreams then end, as when the film is no longer projected onto the screen? Or do their dreams just change in appearance, taking on new light and colors? Is this perceptible in any way to the one who dreams?

My dear Unnur is dead. She died in a dream one night when no one was near. Blessed be her memory.

Personally, I'm in decent enough shape, not counting the stiffness in my shoulders and knees. Old Lady Age is doing her job. Of course, there are moments when you look at your slippers and think how the day will come when the slippers will be standing there—but not you yourself to put them on. But, "welcome to it, when it comes," as Hallgrímur Pétursson says in his hymn about death. Enough life has sloshed through my chest. I've had my taste of it—life. That's how it is, dear Helga.

Oh, I've become a compulsive old man—it's clear in how I've started opening old wounds. But everyone has a door. And everyone wants to let his inner person out that door. And my door—it's the old one on my departed father's sheep shed, where the sun shines in through the chinks, long and slender rays between the thin planks. If life exists somewhere, it must be in the chinks. My door has become so crooked and thin and worn out that it's no longer able to hold the inner from the outer. And maybe that's precisely what's good about the carpenter—that he's not perfect? That in his work there are cracks and chinks, letting in sunshine and life.

Soon I'll set off for the Great Relocation congenital to all men, dear Helga. And it's inevitable that people try to lighten their burdens before setting off on such a journey. Of course, it's quite beside the point writing you this letter now, when everyone is more or less dead or senile, but I've decided to jot it down anyway. If you don't like these scrawls of mine, just toss them out. My words are well meant. I've never wished you anything but good—you know that, dear Helga.

Your Hallgrímur died in late winter. His last year, he couldn't swallow any longer because of the cancer; they couldn't get any food into him, that giant of a man. He wasted away in their hands at the hospital, and was nothing but skin and bones when I visited him in February. It was sad to see. Blessed be his memory.

Blessed be all things, indeed, that try and have tried to exist.

My nephew Marteinn fetched me from the retirement home, and I get to spend midsummer in a room with a view of the farm where you and Hallgrímur once lived. I let my mind wander over the slopes all around here, smelling sweetly of long-past sunshine. That's the most one can do these days.

Unnur lay on her deathbed for five years, four and a half of which she wished to die. In many ways, I came out of that period badly. Nor do I understand what came over her. Little by little, it was as if the good in her was overturned and replaced with reprimands about trivialities. If I spilled juice or bumped into a flower vase while I nursed her, I was scolded for having always been a "damned bungler," "incapable of any chores." Might this have been the hardened disposition that existed deep down inside her, but that until then I'd only caught glimpses of?

She stopped getting out of bed and refused to eat, emaciated as she was; she just lay there wasting away due to some invisible sorrow. That familiar old spirit of hers rotted away. Yes, her spirit left her. She grew sharp-tongued and temperamental, no matter how carefully she was coddled. She simply became decrepit, and terribly ill to boot. And the ill may not be judged the same as the healthy. I watched the blue of her eyes grow dim and blacken like the sky over the mountains and felt as if I should be there to provide her company, considering her circumstances. It seemed that she was unhappy with her situation, unhappy having been brought forth into this life, and unhappy at how she'd spent it. For my pains, I was declared an absolute villain who had played a game of deception with her our entire life together. I had never loved her, she said. Ice cold. And then she looked away.

I was as affectionate to her as could be. Bought her newspapers and boxes of chocolates. Brought out photos of her and me in the haymaking at Grundir, of the old farm, of the fish racks bending beneath lumpfish and half-dried cod, of us gathering eiderdown and young puffins on the islets, of me scraping a seal-pup skin and making repairs on the dory in the shed, of Unnur on the Farmall with the milk box on the back, and simply all of the sunshine that I managed to photograph during my life with the old Polaroid camera. We caught a glimpse of you in one of the photos. It was from before Hulda was born, when we did the haymaking together. She pointed at you. Said, "You should have taken her. Not a gelded yearling like me. You always wanted her, not me."

She pushed the album away. She stared at the foot of the bed with empty eyes. I felt for her. Felt that I loved this helpless, feeble old woman, this doomed individual who had almost no one else in the world. I felt that I'd done right tending our small farm with her all those years. Who else would have cared for her? Tears ran down her cheeks like tiny waves of sorrow. Outside our retirement home, night had come and the traffic had started to settle down. The glimmer of a streetlight peeked in through the room's window and shone faintly on her tear-moistened cheeks.

Then she died. In the middle of the night. In a dream.

2

The old ghost that I thought had been put to rest long ago appeared again in Unnur. The specter that folk in our corner of the countryside had conjured up out of sheer irascibility. Wasn't it Hallgerður who awoke in her, that damned Icelandic habit of never being able to shake off the past or forgive anything? At the retirement home, I'd become "an adulterer," "a charlatan," "a downright double-dealer," and she started expounding for me in small details the lustful pleasures that I supposedly had from you every roundup. It left me shamefaced, to put it mildly, and it was sheer grace that there were few to hear it when she started shouting about my taking you from behind, giving your heavy breasts a voracious feel and jerking you so hard that your ass cheeks smacked. That's how she talked: "your heavy breasts." These fits of hers would then end in sobs, with her accusing herself of being a gelded, abandoned yearling. And although she called me a lazybones who could never manage anything financially or domestically—you know, Helga, that I never stopped working, except during the one week that I was laid up with pneumonia—this hurt me less than the accusations of that countryside rumor from so long ago, which threw salt in my wounds.

What was the incident that ignited the rumor but that never took place, yet led to consequences just as bad—no, even worse!—than if the incident had actually occurred? And is it possible to draw a line between what in fact happened and what the slanderous populace says happened, hanging around their kitchens, all worked up from great gulps of coffee, innuendo, and their blather about others? What didn't occur that Feast of St. Lambert, 1939—yet still occurred in the minds of the blatherers?

Was it when the others had made their way down Hörgsdalur Valley and rounded Framneshæð Hill that I supposedly made my way slowly down the ridge and met you in the grassy hollow by

Steinhúsbakkar Slope? And then, so the rumor goes, we walked together and talked about how beautiful the sheep's wool was when they came down from the mountain that year, how the lambs' paunches were white as snow, how plump they were, how clean their lines. And I, as Hay Officer for Hörgár Parish, declared I had no need to fear that farmers would be half starving their sheep that year, so well the haymaking had gone. And then—oh yes—I remembered your mark: double half-cropped tip, low-notched, and swallowtailed both sides. And you asked me what mine was again: cropped and notched upper side left, swallowtailed at the tip and upper side right. Precisely. Then of course we exchanged a few words about the ram Bassi, whom we'd borrowed from out east in Fljót: how barrel-chested he was, how muscular at the spine. And after exchanging these words about Bassi, our blood churned in a sweet frenzy, and I brushed aside your curls and likened them to snow blowing down a mountain slope, but you laughed and said, "Oh, Bjarni!"

Then I supposedly kissed you, and some sort of overexcited groping took place before I pulled down my trousers as you lifted your sweater and bared your breasts, and next I let my milk-white thighs slap against yours as the whimbrel trilled and the heavy scent of heather saturated the air around us, and we two—scrubby beasts, there in the hollow—became one with the dying

growth for a moment or two, and the white seed trailed gelati-
nously from your inner thigh down to some blades of withered
grass that had become the only witnesses to the sudden blaze that
engulfed us.

No less than all of that, apparently.

Is there anything more natural than for such a thing to have
occurred? Hasn't all of creation arranged it so that such chance
meetings might indeed take place?

And folk would have made their kitchen insinuations, as is
their wont. But that wouldn't have done any harm, because I
would have been modest and begged my Unnur humbly for for-
giveness for this wild aberrance, and she doubtlessly would have
dealt with it better than my own repulsive defensiveness, which
would have made enemies of all who wished to hurt me after the
rumor was spread. I would have even tried to make up for it by
lavishing her with even greater tenderness, and understood that
this earthly life isn't about slapping against others' bellies but
about affection and caring for the people closest to you. You and
I would have made love and satisfied our lust, thereby putting it
out of the picture and allowing me to turn to other matters, to
start thinking of and desiring other things.

The fact is it didn't happen. We weren't together up in the
valley, as those who spread this rumor thought—you know that

we just happened to return from the search last and met at the
gap above the corral. That's why we walked together down the
slope. But it was enough to spark an incident in people's minds,
with accompanying sighs and contented exhalations—and who
can fight against it once a person's head starts filling with such
ideas? And so the rumor of our lustful release spread like wildfire,
until the gossip reached my own house. I stepped in one day
from the spring's biting cold and rubbed my hands together and
sighed. "This cold we're having is unheard of," I said as I walked
into the kitchen where Unnur was stooping over her pots.

"Why don't you go fuck to warm up—I'm sure she's waiting
for you with her legs spread on the other side."

Her statement stunned me at first. And then I was furious.
I slapped Unnur's face and told her to guard her tongue. She
reddened. Then she started wailing crazily and called herself a
frigid wretch and said she didn't understand why I was holding
onto her. It would be best if I cut her loose. That I loved you and
not her.

I said no.

She said it would be best if I left her and took you as my wife
instead. She said that she'd seen how I looked at you, and that I
never looked at her like that. That I coveted you. Then she rushed

off and shoved herself into the closet. I said, "No. That will never happen!"

She shouted out from the closet and wept pent-up tears that she actually seemed to be fighting against, making her weeping even more poignant to hear. I sat there as if thunderstruck on the master bed. Stared down at the floor. Started thinking about whether I shouldn't try to polish up the damned floorboards. The cursed boards were starting to peel and crack and could easily put a splinter in someone's foot.

I was heavyhearted after the cruel slander started spreading around the district; or, shall I say, the cruel slander soon felt like a big air bubble around my heart. I was discontent in my daily occupations, grouchy and impatient, and didn't know where to direct what was surging within me. I felt as if people were looking at me suspiciously. "Damned adulterer," I read in the glances of my neighbors when I went to the Co-op or to church. Unnur grew distant from me, perhaps because I'd grown insolent and irritated at her sobbing at home.

Inside me, a bug sparked to life, longing to spray its digestive juices on the sweet event that was on everyone's lips, but which I'd never gotten to experience, though my name was attached to it. I began to desire you, dear Helga. It's just how you were created; it was no wonder they started spreading the rumor. In doing so, they revealed their own dreams.

Every time I came to visit you and Hallgrímur to loan you worm or stool medicine or do whatever else a friend, neighbor, and hay officer could, and Hallgrímur was in the Eastfjords, "breaking in something more than a mare," as you put it, leaving you alone on the farm with your two children, my thoughts were primitive. God alone knows how paltry I was in my soul after news of this nonevent spread; I was bitter at being convicted, without having sipped of the cleansing sweetness of the crime.

I s it any wonder that I thought of you whenever they went to herd the sheep up in Fellir? Have I said that I felt as if I'd fallen into a heavy whirlpool after the rumor started going around? The autumn that we met following the other herders down Mógilsbakki Hill. It was Ingjaldur of Hóll who first started running his tongue about us getting together, I know it. Who was he to blather and make insinuations about others? There's a famous line attributed to his father, Guðmundur, from the time when two families lived at Hóll and it was so crowded that everyone shared the same bed in the family room. Guðmundur supposedly said the following to Bárður's wife as she snuggled up to him one evening: "Oh, is that you, Sigríður? But then who's Bárður banging?" You don't suppose that was the night when Ingjaldur was conceived?

When my mind wanders back to those times, I think unabashedly of our relationship, which began to bloom shortly after the slander started getting to me. You might say I've become completely immoral, like a shameless ladies' man. But I remember feeling as if I wanted to let everything bottled up inside me burst forth. On you.

Little by little the distance between Unnur and me grew, as we shared no intimacy to speak of. She was always there, of course, doing her work steadily, with an expression for everything: "First to droop is the reddest rose," she said about my wise idea of sending the biggest lambs to the slaughterhouse first, to be butchered, barreled, salted down, and sold to Norway. "Well then—angels watch me" meant "I'm going to bed now." "Beams and motes," she declared, when something was said about the folk at Hóll or the neighboring farms. As if you could never say anything! Our conversations grew awkward. Her entire demeanor became mechanical and predictable, like the spinning jenny that she worked in her spare time. A rhythmic, clapping beat. She always said the same things, in her own way, passionless. She was a fit farmwoman and was tremendously good at distinguishing sheep, meaning she knew which heads belonged to which lambs, even after they'd been singed and boiled. And there was a kind of thread connecting us, though quite tangled. She made blood pudding for the winter, did salting and curing (until the freezer arrived), made jam, and smoked meat and fish most industriously. It's rare for a woman to be in charge of the smoke sheds, but I couldn't get anywhere near them, apart from helping with the salting and other preparations. Except for the lumpsucker, which was my job alone. Anything other than work was the most despicable waste of time in her eyes.

Once some visitors came: Finnur Fowler, as he was called, with his four sons, who, like him, all turned out to have the greatest talent for hunting seabirds and rappelling down cliffs for their eggs. I recall that Finnur had no more tobacco, and it was all sold out at the Co-op. We went to the barn, and I picked leaves from the hay for him; these he stuck in his pipe and subsequently looked as happy as could be as he sipped coffee and sucked on his pipe in the kitchen. This was an old trick, and for our own amusement we came up with a new expression: "Hay—tobacco for hard times." Then the Co-op started selling Commander cigarettes, and after that breakthrough Finnur was never seen smoking anything else. In fact, it was Finnur Fowler who taught me to smoke Commanders. But anyhow, Finnur asked me all about the activities of the Reading Club, for which I was the book buyer. We were reading *Sturlunga saga* then, and I gave him an idea of what was discussed in the reading circle; for instance, when Gissur saved himself by hiding in the whey tub. This inspired heated debate over whether such a thing could actually have happened, or whether the account of the burning was exaggerated later. For some reason, this chafed Unnur so much that every time I went to a meeting of the Reading Club, I was, according to her, going to discuss "Gissur in the whey tub." Whenever I went up to the garret to read recently arrived books that I'd ordered from Reykjavík, she asked what was new of Gissur in the whey tub when I came back down; it was always the same old refrain every time books came up, as if culture and literature were unnecessary luxuries that you should be ashamed of giving your attention, because in the meantime you were neglecting your work.

They had no inclination for books, her forefathers in Blöndudalur Valley. They were more for the body than the soul and wanted only to work. Not every story about them was generous. Her grandfather was long renowned for fining a female worker on his farm fifty aurar for dropping the chamber pot and wasting the old urine. That's how precious this liquid was to them, while human relationships were of little value. And while I'm on the subject of the folk in Blöndudalur, there's another story about when her mother was baking bread. Once folk there thought the bread tasted funny. Finally someone said straight out that the bread definitely tasted like piss, and others agreed. The housewife wondered aloud whether she'd grabbed the wrong pail when she mixed the dough. She took a bite and chewed for a long time before saying, "Well, darned if I know what that is."

Now I've lost the thread, Helga. But I've lost it for a reason. I actually feel bad bringing this up.

Naturally, I knew that there was more going on in Unnur to explain this distracted behavior of hers, which seemed to be saying just one thing: *I'm guilty.*

I understood her and sympathized with her.

I knew that after the operation it was as if work became her sole raison d'être. She was punishing herself for another problem that was impossible for her to discuss frankly. She was suppressing her misery, and sorrow devours the heart, as it says in the *Hávamál*. She wouldn't seek help. Nothing could persuade her. She either screamed and sobbed in a closet while I stared, paralyzed, at the knots in the floorboards, or she disappeared behind the spinning jenny and doggedly drove the spindles.

I can tell you a little story to explain this a bit. Sometime after she had her operation, it became clear that our cow had mastitis. The milk turned to curds or cheese in the left udder. There had to be an explanation for this, and I racked my brains over it until I discovered the cause one day when I was rigging a fishing line on the other side of the cowshed gable. Unnur didn't know I was there.

She started milking our Huppa as usual, but after a few moments I heard grumbling and swearing, and when I took a closer look I saw her prodding and punching the cow's udder with half-clenched fists, cursing and calling the creature bad names since it wouldn't give her milk as quickly and willingly as she wanted. I couldn't stand for this and burst in and gave her a piece of my mind there in the cowshed. She kicked at the pail in a huff and ran out, choking down sobs.

But I was a good husband to her, have no doubt of that. I asked again and again whether she would like to talk about what had happened, whether we could consult the experts down south. But she wouldn't budge.

She abandoned me in the physical world. Doubtless, any caresses only reminded her of what she was no longer capable of, and for that reason she tried to avoid sparking my desire. The shame bent her humanity. I could never so much as hint at the operation or suggest that it might be possible to go back to the doctors for another operation that could put the first one right. It was clear as day that this medical procedure had gone horribly wrong. But it was as if she took the doctors' mistake as a predetermined and immutable fate—as if she deserved nothing else. Her reaction was always the same whenever I mentioned the operation. First she would stuff herself into the closet and weep and wail, then pale like withered grass and speak not a word. Eventually the redness would return to her cheeks and she would start cranking the spinning jenny so hard that the spindles smoked. She could work like that long into the night. I stopped bringing it up because of her reaction. But I'd lived long enough and had enough sense to know that doctors make mistakes. Everyone makes mistakes. Otherwise we aren't human.

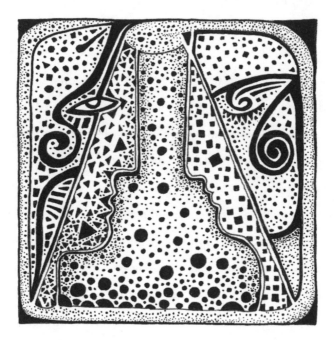

4

Then came the December day when I helped you with servicing the ewes. I came as agreed with my ram, Kútur, the treasure of the Jökuldalur stock. I recall that it took place on the Feast of St. Ambrose, and my coveralls smelled of glycerol after repairing Gauti of Staður's International the day before.

You dove straight into speaking badly of Hallgrímur, who was busy with "the mares to the east." It was obvious you two were having troubles as well. Hallgrímur put too much of the farming on your shoulders and displayed you too little tenderness when he was near. Yes, I must tell it as it is: he wasn't much of a farmer, that Hallgrímur, and not his father's son at all. There are loads of stories about his father, old Jónas, who cultivated more than a few hayfields at his farm, Alviðra, and whose grass was said to grow better than any other farmer's.

Of course, I helped you with the breeding that short, snowless winter day; I always tried to be there for you, both as a friend and the hay officer for Hörgár Parish. I made my way lazily down the track by the sea on the old Farmall with Kútur in the trailer—over the Lambeyrar sandbanks and along the hard, dry grassland that was only lightly covered with snow up to the Skorar crags. Past Blóðbrekka Slope, where it's said that a teenage boy in the Middle Ages cut his own throat and let himself bleed to death. The creeping thyme winds around the rocks there, and every time I pass by the place I'm overcome with a deep-rooted weariness.

I looked out at Barnasker Skerry, where eagles, of old, ate small children at their ease after nabbing them from their homefields, while mothers screamed on the shore and no boat could push past the breakers. Who hasn't heard the children's shrill wails coming from those skerries through the fog and north wind? Then I meandered past Freyjaskjól, where, without any warning, men grow erect and women aroused as they pass by alone—it being an old stopover where children were eagerly conceived. There under the spell of these old places I drove slowly and thought of you. Was that perhaps the point of no return? Next, I drove down the gully and over Þröngubotnalækur Stream, that useless trickle, which since ancient times marked the boundary between the farms, and therefore between us. If it hadn't been for the stream, all the land up to the Víðines River would have belonged to Kolkustaðir; there would have been no Alviðra, and no Hallgrímur, because his father Jónas wouldn't have lived there, nor his father Kristinn before him. It would have been just you and I, Helga. And Kolkustaðir.

The wind was from the north, and sunbeams shone between tongues of sleet hanging from banks of storm clouds. Under such weather conditions, there should have been more ram lambs that year. You called this superstitious and wouldn't let me forget it when your ewes produced far more ewe lambs. After Kútur had finished tupping the ready ewes and licked the salt in the back pen, I recall how you came over to me and leaned forward on the rail, showing the outline of your white bosom. I felt the ewes to assess their body condition, as is the hay officer's responsibility. I sank my fingers into the thick, coarse wool; felt the amplitude of their chests and from there down along the ribs to the rib tips, finding no flaws. Then I turned to their backs and felt down along the loins and then the rump to check for any gauntness. Next I ran my fingers along the breastbone, and from there up onto the spinous processes and down along the transverse processes as you watched carefully and rubbed your nipples, those beautiful knots on the female trunk, against the trough rail. I felt the thick, muscular legs down to the hocks and saw that this sheep was well rounded and well fed, removing any doubt that they would all stand the winter. But you leaned forward, giving a glimpse of one breast, and said casually that I was a great genius in touching and feeling, and asked whether I knew how to use such a gentle touch on the female kind.

"Well," I said, "it looks to me as if you're fairly well rounded yourself," and before I knew it I'd reached my hand in jest toward your chest; but just as I made this silly gesture you bared your breast, heavy and swelling, and told me to look, apparently in full earnest. I noticed the blush spread over your cheeks. Yet it wasn't shame, but rather pure fire—it was the gleam of fire. Isn't it so, Helga?

A pervasive, all-encompassing fleshly desire overcame me seeing your bare body in this place; it had been a long time since I'd laid eyes on such a finely fashioned, wholesome form. Your encouraging words enflamed me so strongly that I had to go out

into the north wind to cool down, wandering around the farmyard like an old ram pulled off a willing ewe in the heat of things.

But I held firm. God alone knows what a heavy burden that
was. When summer came, I cooled off in the brook out back of
the farm, stripping bare and trying to extinguish the fire in my
flesh by bathing in the chilly water. I composed a sacred verse
that I showed to no one, except you, now, because you inspired it:

> *When she loves*
> *O'er mountaintops it rings.*
> *She bathes her silky hair*
> *In clear mountain springs.*

Trying to cool myself in the water had the opposite effect. Before I
knew it, I found myself most brutishly masturbating, for which I
was ashamed, feeling, as I always did, as if someone could see me.
That I was doing something wrong. Why does one think this way?
Much later, I realized that what I sensed was naturally the hidden
people in the Fólkhamrar crags above the brook. Do you suppose
they find it amusing watching us wretched humans pleasuring
ourselves? Maybe they feel sorry for us, trapped in our lust?

I realized that I would never succeed in getting you out of
my mind—I would covet you as long as I drew breath. It doesn't

bother me to write this, Helga, I'm an old man who has nothing to lose. Soon all of my fire will be extinguished as I lie there
gaping with my mouth full of brown earth. Is it possible I'll still
covet you then? Maybe I'll be a ghost and wander around with
my dick hanging out, trying to express myself?

You sparked in me a desire that grew and could burst into a
bonfire at any moment and for no reason. If I saw a stout tussock
or a rounded grassy bank, your lines would combine with it in
my mind until I could no longer distinguish the world in and of
itself—only you in the world's manifestations. When I saw a ram
lamb greedy for nourishment from its mother, I saw myself in it.
How does the old rhyme go?

> *Cross the road ran little ram,*
> *Lost and bleating for his mam,*
> *To help her find her straying lamb.*

It's of course only I who knows the location of the "Helga
Tussocks" here in this district, and when I die I'll take this place-
name with me to the grave. These tussocks on the south side of
the slope at Göngukleif resemble earthly casts of your breasts,
albeit in enlarged form; it's as if the shape of the tussocks, with
their smooth, flat tops and steep, rounded sides, are made from

the same mold as your breasts, by the same creative hands. How often did I lie there in the Helga Tussocks in a sunny, southwesterly wind, with my head between the breasts, imagining that I was in your arms? At the same time, you rode naked on a black horse through my mind, and I watched your breasts bob slowly to the rhythm of the trot. Or you stood there like the ogress Gjálp in *Snorri's Edda*: astride the river, causing it to rise so much that I floated carefree in your warm, fragrant stream. And there I lay, the man whom every resident of the parish looked upon as your deceiver, which created a sort of pressure that forced its way into my will and made me simply covet you more. Yet I held firm.

I recall that the weather was exceptionally bad that season: there was a bitter, chilling north wind, making it impossible for me to travel up the fjord with Unnur's skyr. I left as soon as it relented, with all the tubs full of frozen skyr. And wouldn't you know it—the northerly turned into a southwesterly gale, blowing straight at me and churning water into the boat. This was shortly after I elevated the dory's boards and bought a little Gauti motor for it, on which I let it run—otherwise I would have vanished into the deep that day. I bailed desperately and steered into the wind at the same time, fighting my way like that up the fjord for hours on end. I remember what I was thinking; yes, I can say it now: it was pretty much all the same to me if I sank, but worse was the fact that we'd never been intimate. That was the only drink in this mortal life I regretted never having sipped— it's perhaps like this: a man's desire, constantly suppressed in his breast, appears brighter and clearer in the face of death. Nor did my lustful desire exactly slacken afterward, when I looked over at your farm.

"Fresh Unfrozen Kolkustaðir Skyr," wrote shopkeeper Jens on a board that he hung up as an advertisement at the Co-op. Folk chuckled about old Jensi's logic for quite some time afterward.

5

Then came the spring when your sheep got the scab, and you called on me to help with the Walz's dip. It was the spring that our Member of Parliament didn't come, which he'd always done before the elections. We discussed this out in front of the Co-op. Gunnar of Hjarðarnes asked whether it wouldn't be best to vote for someone else since the Progressive Party's MP no longer showed his face in the district.

"You believe in God even though you can't see him," said Gísli of Lækur, before blowing his nose vigorously into his handkerchief. At that the matter was settled.

Hallgrímur was up north breaking in horses, and your kids were at boarding school. You were alone. On the farm. I'd received clear instructions from the Farmers' Association on how to deal with the sheep scab, depending on whether it was from sheep ked or mites. Hörgár Parish had at its disposal a so-called portable bathtub, paid for by the district administration and easy to move on custom-made wooden posts that we called litters for fun. The parish had a huge lant can—eighty liters of stinking, concentrated cow's urine purchased from elsewhere—and a big aluminum pot. I brought them to you on the hay wagon. It was a slushy spring day, and the brooks trickled like silver threads down all the slopes. I was always considered eccentric and followed my own lead when it came to raising sheep. I didn't want to squander old lore concerning the furtherance and fortification of sheep farming. Clear instructions came from Reykjavík about using the lant diluted with water for the dip, but I preferred to follow Sheriff Magnús Ketilsson's lant-dip formula, which called for tossing both seaweed and wood ashes into the undiluted lant and then adding tar, old human urine, and several tobacco leaves. Which made all the difference. We made this mix and heated it in the fireplace of your old farmhouse, and after we'd poured it all into the good old portable bathtub in the middle of the sheep shed, we dipped the sheep in it. You doubtless remember as well as I how it went. The mix splashed onto your blouse when you tried to rub the liquid into the wool, while I tried to hold the ewes to make sure it didn't flood their noses and mouths.

In my mind's eye I can vividly envision the moment when I poured the shark-liver oil over the spines of the final lambs. Then I see you starting to remove your blouse, and the light from the little window where the medicines stood falls on your breasts, creating shadows in the hollows beneath.

I beheld your loins filling out from your waist and I grew completely stiff as my eyes drank in this image. I'd never witnessed a fairer earthly sight except when I was berrying up on Kúluholt Hill one late August; I looked over the countryside, barren down to the hillocks and gravel beds, but then saw how the freshly mown hayfields of Tungunes were bedecked with dense, radiant-green, ripened hay—the three hectares that I'd plowed and sown on my Farmall, which I'd purchased through the association, the first to do so in the district. This green patch was like ivory in oak, as was said of Þórr when he came among other men, this patch that I should never actually have needed to cultivate, since I'd never used the hay from Tungunes myself; no,

I gathered it all into a stack three to four ells high and eighteen to twenty ells long and draped a sail over it, to be used as a reserve in case anyone should be short of hay in late winter. There were sure to be plenty in the community with little hay left over in the spring; that much I knew as hay officer. And just as expected, the Tungunes hay reserve dwindled down, until nothing was left by winter's final days but the staked-down sail. Not a single person said a word of thanks to me, though I kept the Tungunes hay in reserve every autumn for seventeen years. So it went. "Bleeding is the heart that begs," says the old poem, and they perhaps didn't want to admit that they were dependent on someone else, these people. But I was dependent on you. I realized that then, as you stood in the light of the little window, white as a hen salmon newly run to the riffle, smelling of lant and tobacco leaves.

Then the barrier broke within me and everything poured out as if from a pump. I told you what had happened with Unnur. That she'd been sent south for an examination after experiencing pain in her womb for some time. The doctors suspected a tumor in her uterus and determined that the only option was to remove it, although we still hadn't had any children. They tore into her with their instruments and cut out her uterus, Unnur had told me in a choked-up voice.

Had they asked her what she wanted?

No, she wasn't allowed a word in edgewise; no one asked her anything, and she was alone there at the hospital, terrified, because I couldn't leave the animals.

Several months after the operation, when she was supposed to have been healed and I went to check on her, it turned out that she'd been stitched up in such a way that her nether regions couldn't be touched without her experiencing intense pain. That's how they'd left her, those damned white coats. Sewn up so tightly inside that nothing could get in there. Lucky they didn't just suture it all shut! Those were difficult days. She felt so ashamed that burning tears poured from her eyes.

Once she ran out onto the homefield in her nightgown, crying out in a kind of fit of rage, with me following in only my boots and long underwear. What was I to say to her? It might have appeared that I was threatening her and she was fleeing my brandished knife, while what in fact happened was that I'd foolishly mentioned the operation after we'd gone to bed. Luckily no one was looking out the window that night. That I can tell you.

I told you that I'd suggested she let other doctors examine her to find out if this could be fixed, but it didn't make any difference. She gave me an earful. Said that I could slaughter her like any other gelded yearling. Got into the bedroom closet and started sobbing so loudly that all the rafters creaked. And I stared bewilderedly at the knots. Never in my life had I witnessed such behavior.

And then you said it, as I lamented these things at your breast. It wasn't the words themselves that enflamed me, but rather how you said it; in the heavy, sweet scent of stale urine you pressed my head to your bosom, your holy tussocks, and said softly, deeply, like a draft through a gully: "Love her—through me."

Love her through you! And then you drove my head into your heavy breasts—and what man could have withstood such treatment?

Maybe you'll find it crude of me to bring this up, to put it in words to you, my dear Helga. Reputation, respect, it's all the same to me. What's a man to do with such things when all is said and done? When it comes right down to it, I'd have to admit that I can't recall ever knowing any such earthly bliss as during our lovemaking there in the barn that eternal spring day. When I finally got the chance to touch your smooth curves and drown in the fullness of your lips during that joyous, fleeting rut of my life. What happened, happened. I pulled down my trousers, and you shucked off every piece of clothing and bared your breasts and triangular tuft and ran into the barn with me after you, so exceptionally aroused and lustful. Your body trembled and quivered

beneath me in the hay pile. It was like touching life itself. You
moaned so loudly that I was afraid it could be heard at the farm,
but I didn't care. I couldn't have given a damn even if the entire
slanderous parish of Hörgár came to the barn door drooling and
slobbering to witness plain as day what we were up to there in
the hay. How your breasts undulated like surging white ground
swells beneath your skin. A fairer sight I have never seen. For
which I'd waited so long.

I hitched up my trousers. Spoke not a word. Looked away.
You said I shouldn't be ashamed. Smiled blissfully as if you didn't
know what a sin was. Sat up on your elbow with straw in your
hair and said heartily that such things happened on the best
of farms, and smiled and sought my eyes for assent. You were
impeccable there in the hay. I poured out the bathtub's contents
and bore it out to the hay wagon. Put on my balaclava and started
up the tractor. Puttered my way down the old road by the sea so
as not to risk meeting anyone. My inner thighs sticky. The lant
vat on the back of the wagon and my soul spun and twisted like
a ghost in a washing machine.

It never happened. This had never taken place. That's how
my soul responded to the onslaught of the flesh. My body had
become meek, but my soul hardened! No one was ever to dis-
cover that the rumor had been confirmed. My heart ached that

night, feeling of course that I'd betrayed my Unnur and it was an ugly thing to do—my body knew it. But I'd also been given a glimpse through the doorway to heaven.

Yet as paradoxical as it might sound, it was as if the rumor ceased after it became a reality. As if the slander had been a shout of encouragement from the natural will that desired our union. Yes, mightn't the will of creation have found a mouthpiece in the slanderous windpipes of the parish? And then fallen silent as soon as it was released. I actually found it easier to be among my neighbors afterward. As if I'd fulfilled their will. Damned if Unnur didn't simply look a bit more relaxed. It wasn't so dangerous, then.

Several weeks passed. I put everything I had into being loving to Unnur and didn't mention the operation, and she neither hid in the closet nor shouted to the rafters that she was a gelded yearling that would be best slaughtered. Everything settled down somehow as if after a storm. Beloved be all that settles down, and beloved be human kindness. I'm out in the sheep shed feeding the sheep. Your loins are silhouetted against the hay trough. Your breasts are tossed about in the hay. Your blissful moans resound in the silo. Your eyes are in the pleading, hungry eyes of the ewes. I look at the spiderweb in the window where a sunbeam plays on a blowfly's shimmering green. But I don't see it. I don't see anything. Except for your simmering white loins, your veins with their ever-present thirst, and your breasts staring at me from the knots in the barn walls. Everywhere I see you in my mind's eye, with the same "mental vigor" that sheep are said to have in old breeding booklets.

Then it was time for the required annual dips, and I started becoming your regular caller, as Katla in *Eyrbyggja saga* might have said.

T he next year was the most glorious I ever lived. The year
that I have called the rut of my life. It snowed a great deal
that winter; exceptionally severe frosts crusted the drifts,
and pack ice lined the northern coasts. Under these conditions,
between Christmas and New Year, old Sigríður from up north
in Hólmanes kicked the bucket; the Grim Reaper didn't choose
the most convenient time for his assault. "When the call comes,
no one buys his way out," as Hallgrímur said. I recall that the
sorrow over this loss gave way entirely to concerns over how on

earth we were supposed to bury the old woman. Though folk often say how tough it is to live in those northerly parts in the winter, it's a sight worse to die there. Jósteinn of Karlsey and I were given the task of retrieving the body and bringing it to church.

We took Jósteinn's boat over on the day before New Year's Eve. There was a northerly swell but calm weather as we set out for the place that the wags call the backside of beyond and which at the time had neither a road nor a decent landing. A proper road to the place wasn't constructed until after it was deserted—as strange as that sounds. It's no wonder that the Hólmanes farm was the first to be abandoned in our parish; the hayfields there are quite small and exposed to the open sea. But despite the straitened conditions, love always flourished between Sigríður and Gísli. Visiting them made me think of the old couple on the moorland farm in Halldór Laxness's *World Light*, toiling in poverty for forty years. They were like two of the same stamp. People make fun of the most miserly of farms, saying they lie beyond the bounds of civilization, but mightn't it be that there was more civilization found there than anywhere else?

Old Gísli brewed coffee and even added a drop or two of spirits. We talked there in the kitchen about the day to day—whether the lambs had gotten the scours, the agenda of the

Progressive Party, and the last parish council meeting. I took the opportunity and inspected the hay and assessed the sheep and still recall the handsome horn-growth on Gísli's ewes.

Then we said a few "yessirs" and "well nows." As we were leaving, I kept feeling as if we were forgetting something, though I couldn't determine what. We stood out in front of Gísli's farmhouse and watched the murky clouds approach from the north, tongues of sleet licking the surface of the sea, and saw the waves breaking out at Hvalsker Skerry; a gale was clearly blowing in. It also looked as if the boat were about to slip from the landing, which provided only a little shelter from northwesterlies; so, Jósteinn and I said our hasty good-byes and hurried down to it, although I still felt as if I were forgetting something. The feeling, however, was quickly pushed aside, because we had to work fast to avoid being stuck at old Gísli's or lose the boat on the rocks.

After we'd rowed out with the wind somewhat and put more than half the fjord behind us, Jósteinn lets out a horrendous shout! Then he gives me something of an astonished look, sitting there on his thwart, and says, "We forgot the old woman!"

But there was no way to turn back, what with the waves breaking on both sides. We agreed that Sigríður hadn't wanted to leave her beloved husband and made herself invisible in order not to—well, at least in our minds. When we asked Gísli in the spring whether it had slipped his mind as well, he replied that he simply hadn't had the faintest idea that the wet and wind from the north would last so long. So polite was Gísli that in our agitated rush when we realized the wind was blowing in, he couldn't bring himself to interrupt us and remind us of why we'd come.

After this famous corpse-forgetting trip of ours, there came such exceptionally fierce, freezing gales from the north—absolutely monstrous, thought most—that it was impossible to go north by boat for months on end. By late March this started weighing heavily on us, since it was Jósteinn and I who forgot the body and were responsible for its transportation; the matter was raised at a parish council meeting, and we were finally allotted a motorboat with a dinghy and a captain from down south in Hólar Parish. This time, four of us from the parish council went to fetch blessed Sigríður: Jósteinn, Hjörtur, Gunnar of Hjarðarnes, and I, and we cast anchor in Helguvík, which is considerably south of Hólmanes and decently protected from the ocean waves. We rowed ashore in the dinghy, four men in long underwear, knee-high wool socks, and winter scarves. We landed at Sandvík, walked up the beach, and then inland toward Hólmanes. The weather was tolerable, though I recall that there was a considerable amount of blowing, drifting snow; we were relieved to be able to pause at Gísli's fishing huts to brush off the snow and gather our strength before heading up the slope to the farm. The first thing we set eyes on was Sigríður's coffin. Hjörtur asked whether it would be impolite to check whether Sigríður was in the coffin, the dear woman, and in the incredible absence of any odor someone threw out the idea that maybe she'd just held up well in the cold from the north. Hjörtur lifted the lid. The coffin was empty.

"She can't have become a ghost," sighed Jósteinn in his hoarse voice, which always sounded like a distant shout from somewhere up on a heath.

"Listen, mate!" came Gunnar of Hjarðarnes's same old refrain, before he wondered out loud whether Gísli could have found a place to put her in the ground—if he'd buried her without the coffin, he must have put her in a snowdrift; but then Hjörtur suggested we spend no more time there contemplating the coffin, because that wasn't what we came there for. We needed to get back before dark, which wouldn't give us much time if we had to start by digging her up. As the old verse said, "Day gave men barely any precious light."

I recall that Gísli was wearing a spotless white shirt and welcomed us warmly, offering us tasty oatmeal cookies that he'd baked the day before. Naturally, he'd dreamed the future or perceived somehow that we were on our way, long before we arrived. I imagined that that's the way it was. It seemed as if such sensitivity disappeared simultaneous to the spread of the telephone; that this instrument killed real communication between people, the same way that ghosts and spirits seemed to have retreated when people started polluting the air with radio broadcasts and other radio waves. Folk from remote areas who are used to isolation have sharper senses than others. I've read that some tribes in Africa still possess such sensitivity and sense visits from people or animals long beforehand.

Gísli thanked us over and over for sacrificing so much to come back out there, and poured delicious caraway coffee into cups on the covered kitchen table. The weather conditions were the first topic of discussion—such an unparalleled bad spell. Then the condition of lambs, news of the district, the military occupation and whether it wasn't a calamity for the nation, and so on. *I suppose we'll all end up becoming crofters again. Not of chieftains and temple priests or bishops. Of the big foreign nations instead. Yes, just like in the Middle Ages. It would be best to go on the dole immediately. That's what I say. Yes, I'm afraid so. Hmm, most likely.* Then the kitchen fell silent. Delicate whiffs of snow drifted over the frozen gravel bank above the farm.

Hjörtur cut the matter short: "We came up the beach to get here and took a little breather at the fishing huts. We saw the coffin there, and you know what our task is, so we were curious to know whether you'd maybe buried the late Sigríður, or, well, how you might have dealt with this difficult situation that's come up."

"Aw," said old Gísli, "now I wouldn't...say that...I'd already buried her." He spoke hesitantly, sighing now and then, making it difficult to get to the bottom of it. He explained to us that his only option had been to do what he could to try to prepare the body of his Sigríður decently. Then he said, using the common northern term for what elsewhere is called the smokehouse: "I made a little covering for her and tied it with a hempen string and put her up in the rafters...ehhh...in the meat house."

"The meat house?" I shouted involuntarily, and regretted it immediately.

Old Gísli looked even more embarrassed and stared at the floor as he said, all choked up, that he'd seen no other way out, but that he'd had, on the other hand, enough store of fragrant, fine, dry hay for smoking, so he'd just tried to fix things that way.

Then Hjörtur went to him and embraced this forlorn man whom it was so easy to like: "My dear man. That's what I call sorting things out! What a genius idea."

And as everyone was saying nice things about this solution of Gísli's—to smoke the late Sigríður—Hjörtur pulled out a bottle of rum from his winter coat and proposed that we drink a little funeral toast to her.

And I remember as if it were yesterday how moved I was when I went out to the smokehouse and saw how carefully old Gísli had completed his task. I remember that I thought this procedure should be made into a special Icelandic funereal tradition, you know, for when people were grieving their loved ones. How the smoke would help the tears flow. Although it wouldn't be particularly easy to smoke people in Reykjavík. So it would have to be a kind of deluxe countryside tradition. But anyhow. Gísli had built a frame around Sigríður and was careful not to wrap the hempen cord too tightly, allowing the smoke to slip through. He'd dressed her in a coarse burlap sack that also allowed the smoke through and covered her nakedness at the same time. He constructed this cage, rather than a stretcher, in order to make it easier to turn her over on the crossbeam and smoke her body back and front.

We helped him take her down off the crossbeam, and the entire time that we busied ourselves with this, Gísli spoke to his Sigríður as if she were still alive and kicking: "Well, my dear, they've finally come up here to get you. Now you're going to go for a little boat trip, my good woman." That's how he spoke to this woman, whose dead body he'd so affectionately prepared for burial. Gunnar of Hjarðarnes couldn't refrain from saying something that we were naturally all thinking, as we lifted her carefully from the cage and over into the coffin, her skin rosy brown, smelling like the best smoked lamb meat; I swear she had a smile on her face. Gunnar said, "Well, mate, I don't know what you say, but I think Sigríður has never looked better!"

The tears glistened on Gísli's cheeks as he loosely nailed the coffin lid shut again. He'd asked to be allowed to do this himself and spoke constantly to his Sigríður as he did so. Gísli came back with us, and Sigríður's funeral took place the following Sunday.

I don't remember a single word of Reverend Hjálmar's eulogy, but it's certain that no church ceremony smelled as good in my memory as Sigríður's funeral. Gísli was always a model farmer. He never lacked for hay and his ewes generally bore two lambs, were easy to herd, horned and clean. He ran a model farm at Hólmanes after the death of Sigríður, just as before, until he was found dead in the feeding trough, his arms full of hay. That was several years after this story took place. Much later we heard that the gable had blown off the farmhouse in a southwesterly gale, and in the summers hikers were constantly having a look inside. So the farmhouse was torn down and, shortly afterward, the sheep sheds.

Last time I passed by Hólmanes, there was nothing to see there but the fresh green rise where the farmhouse stood. A breeze in the green grass and a memory of people's lives. And that, my dear Helga, will be the fate of our farmsteads as well.

But anyhow, where was I? Yes, I was discussing the rut of my life. While Hallgrímur was off breaking horses, leaving you to wrestle with the farm work and me around to serve you hand and foot, if I might put it that way in doting jest, well, "the road to Steinastaðir wasn't long," as the old verse about Gaukur Trandilsson says. That was the year I reprimanded the farm advisor, telling him in a letter that he should reconsider his grading standards, because Ingjaldur from Hóll's ram was absolutely useless for servicing the ewes.

In the spring, a ram exhibition was held in Eyri. A bright yellow light played over the mountains and a strong, warm west wind blew into the fjord. I wore a shirt and my striped jacket and put my newly carded Kútur in the back of the Land Rover, lit a Commander cigarette, and drove off with a certain expectant feeling. Kútur was the most splendid ram that I have ever owned, you know, Helga, and we certainly used him a lot for breeding. In that we were both at our best, Kútur and I. I'd bought him from down south in Fljót, bred from a champion German ram and with the Jökuldalur bloodline in him as well. Short-horned, broad-muzzled, an exceptionally full loin; his legs were incredibly thick down to his hocks and with an inverted U-shaped twist, providing him a damned stable foothold. His breast had good curvature; his chest was well muscled and wide, meaning his knees didn't knock together when he walked, unlike Ingjaldur from Hóll's rams. His fleece had thick underwool and was free of kemp, the outer coat curly yet moderately coarse; his eyes were dark and lively. He weighed in at a hundred kilos. A large number of people had gathered at Eyri, and there was a lot to discuss out in front of the meeting house. They'd come from deep throughout the Firðir region and from out east in the Tunga district. People chatted about the weather, the scours, the Progressive Party's agenda, the association, and

the military occupation. Blew their noses. Took snuff. A flask
or two was passed around, and Steinar and Bragi, the brothers
from the Eyri farms, recited poetry by Kristján Ólason, that
genius versifier, with such a lovely rhythm, so effortless, their
harmonies softly flowing:

> *Contented soon I make my way*
> *back to the dust whence I arrived.*
> *Long though I toiled with little pay*
> *of life's good gifts was ne'er deprived.*

> *Deep down inside my heart there lay*
> *—same as others gained indeed—*
> *a clew to point to me the way,*
> *though I to it paid little heed.*

> *This life and I o'er wages high*
> *to blows our quarrels often came.*
> *We leave behind now as we die*
> *all burden, debt, demand, and claim.*

Then none other than the farm advisor himself arrived in his
white coat, went down the line of rams, held his tape measure

up to them, and prodded them before they were weighed at the meeting house. I remember feeling fairly confident, thinking that Kútur made a fine show, and several people remarked that it was a magnificent creature I'd acquired. It didn't hurt that his lineage could be traced to both a champion German ram and the Jökuldalur stock.

The advisor had a different opinion. He informed me that Kútur's legs were far too long, but that his chest and back were exceptional. That's what the esteemed advisor said: that Kútur's legs were far too long! Anger boiled within me as he announced at the ceremony up on the ribbon-bedecked platform that Ingjaldur from Hóll's ram was to receive first prize. To make matters worse, he recommended that we on the neighboring farms make greatest use of him during the next servicing.

Ingjaldur's Dindill won only by virtue of having shorter legs. There was no goddamned chest on that knock-kneed, cow-hocked devil! And damned if his horns weren't protruding so much that he couldn't graze on flat ground. I was astounded. That potbelly! Most everyone took umbrage, and the following verse was composed and quickly made the rounds, because the advisor himself was skinny, splay-footed, and gangly to the highest degree:

If of himself the advisor took measure,
no prize he'd gain, no marks he'd notch.

Esteemed, perhaps, yet wrecking the pleasure
are lanky legs from ground to crotch.

The fact was that the land had given birth to geniuses at sheep farming. The first lesson one learned from the old farmers was to have the sheep long-legged, making it possible for them to forage on beaches in the winter and on uneven, tussocky ground. But here we had Mr. Bigshot! A university-educated man who'd learned from books in Reykjavík that sheep should be short-legged, in order to follow some worldly fashion. So people were supposed to service ewes with a ram so short-legged and big-bellied that it toppled onto its back between the first tussocks it ran into! Give me a break. That's how Ingjaldur's rams were. A story about this went around for a long time: once a visitor comes to the farm at Hóll and asks to see Ingjaldur, but a boy answers that his dad isn't at home, that he's out "uprighting the rams."

The thing is, this is how everything that's been built up in Icelandic culture is bungled; folk go abroad and learn some damned rubbish that has nothing to do with Iceland, but try in the name of the latest fashion to do everything they can to spoil and wreck the distinctive features that have developed here. In Italy they eat sparrows. My grandmother Kristín taught me to ask the wagtail in the spring how the future would be, and that you must never steal the wheatear's eggs, because if you did, your fingers would become stiff and twisted. Isn't it nicer to live with such beliefs and take delight in blessed little birds, rather than eat them just to follow some worldly fashion?

Where was I again? Oh, yes. You must remember it better than I, Helga, after we'd ferried the ready ewes down to the dulse-strewn seashore and tried to service them with Ingjaldur's ram. There's an old aphorism that my father said came from the Greek philosopher Aristotle, but I remember how Sheriff Magnús Ketilsson worded it: that the birth of twin lambs was brought about "by the great mental vigor of sheep who behold at once both land and sea the moment the ram releases and the ewe receives the seed." That's how he worded it, the dear man. And for us it paid off.

But there was no way to service the ewes with that fat belly. And that damned monotone bleat of his—such sounds truly get on my nerves. So now the farmers were angry, and we agreed to let Kútur, Bassi, and Klængur service the rest. I wrote a sternly worded letter. Expressed my doubts about the ability of the farm advisor to judge sheep. Said that I didn't want to see my flock ruined by such an unprofitable ram as Dindill, and that this new short-legged sheep craze from the continent had no business at all in our tussocky landscape. And what would be next: were we supposed to start eating sparrows? Besides that, Dindill and the Jökuldalur ewes were too closely related, making him undesirable for propagation (according to Article 4 of the sheep booklet of Hálfdán, Helgi, and Jón, Akureyri, 1855). The sheep farmer (says the same booklet) should choose the best-looking and most well-bred ram, and this Dindill was simply not good looking at all. The creature was badly proportioned. I was sent back an even more sternly worded letter.

I stuck to my guns.

Came in my capacity as Hay Officer to check whether you were still well rounded. Behind the equipment shed we found ourselves a little nook where sunbeams fell through the cracks between the planks, allowing me to assess your body condition precisely in their light. This became our private little joke. You asked me to examine you, and I felt your rib tips, which were free of flaws, and then one rib after another, and the fullness of your back, then your pelvis and legs, down to your hocks, making you quiver like a poplar in the wind; I touched you with eager fingers, conducting a detailed survey of the curvature and amplitude of your breasts. You moaned blissfully. The vision of you naked in the sunbeams was refreshing to the eye, like a blossom on a bare cliff ledge. I really have nothing to compare to this sight. The

best I can think of is when the Farmall arrived, when I pulled the
crate and cardboard off the tractor and beheld the shining glory
that would revolutionize our lives. See how paltry I am in my
mind, dear Helga, likening you, young and naked, to a tractor.
I know I'm just befouling your beauty by comparing you to a
worldly thing. Yet you were a splendid tractor.

God alone knows how I preserved this vision eternally in the
deepest chamber of my heart. I've kept it enshrined. There at the
buzz saw I laid hands on your breasts and sensed their fullness
in the fragrance of the new-mown hay. And the bushy tuft in
pure light. My Kútur and I. We two in the sweet laps of destiny
that life had granted us. When we made love. Your breasts bob-
bing on your rib cage. They were swans on the waves. I let fly
and you moaned ecstatically, and I was soon prepared to slap
my thighs against yours again. So unprecedentedly lustful I
was. I was enamored. I loved everything. My Unnur as well. I
floated like a nacreous cloud through the days. I didn't mind at
all working like a beast, performing both my duties as the parish
hay officer and taking the dory fishing when the time was right,
catching lumpsucker and setting seal-pup nets in the spring for
extra income. I also added onto the sheep shed at that time. I literally leapt out of bed in the mornings. I remember when I boiled

the head of a huge cod that I'd caught in the lumpsucker net.
I sat there in the kitchen, sucking the splendid sweetness from
the bones, my chin glistening with oily broth—and thought that
your kisses were even sweeter, more luscious than this! You were
so close to me when we met briefly in your barn. You with the
heartfelt cordiality that comes so naturally to you alone. You said
that you wanted me and asked whether we shouldn't just run off
together and have done with this district. I laughed and didn't
take you seriously at first. I tried to put words to my emotions,
though I only managed fragments.

Then suddenly it came to an end.

The rut of my life.

Clouds drew over the sun. And it's no secret that a woman who looks at a man the way you did, one autumn evening outside the barn, carries a new life within her. You didn't need to say anything; everything sounded different. It was as if life itself spoke through you. Your heart trembled, weakening your voice. I felt deep sympathy for your anxiety, which naturally threw me off balance. It was as if a wedge had been driven into all my emotions. I was glad to know that I had sparked life and was rueful about the situation—hesitant and speechless—because deep inside, this was precisely what I wanted, to give you a child. The problems arose from our circumstances, with the slanderous tongues of Hörgár Parish out and ready all around us.

There were two choices, you said. They both looked bad to me, you know, dear Helga. You suggested that we say farewell to our lives in the countryside, move south to Reykjavík with your children, and start a new life. There was plenty of work to be had from the Yanks, and inexpensive housing was easy to find. You could get a part-time job as a shop clerk or house cleaner. It would all work out. You couldn't imagine living next to Hallgrímur after your relationship ended. You wanted to leave, and I, Hay Officer for Hörgár Parish, Bjarni Gíslason of the great farmstead of Kolkustaðir, should come with you. In the city we could have a splendid future; the place was loaded with money, and I who was so dexterous and could build whatever it might be, repair any sort of machine, wouldn't have any trouble finding enough to do.

No one there stuck his nose into another's business, you said, unlike in our community. You could take sewing classes and buy material and magazines with patterns, so that you could make your children presentable. People there had manners. There you could study whatever you wanted. You had a dream, you told me. You'd read up on it. You wanted to learn ceramics, you said, and cast clay pots and mugs and art objects. You could go to the theater there and buy yourself a hot cocoa at a café. You could see other plays besides *Skugga-Sveinn*. In Reykjavík, there was no damned eternal, bitter-cold, gusting northern wind from the open ocean, like here. Your enticements were full of excitement and an enthusiasm that I found inspiring, and I smiled, envisioning life in Reykjavík with the luster that you gave it.

Then I remembered who I was.

Where I was.

I turned away and looked at the dung-channel leading out of the sheep shed.

You broke down and started sobbing. You remember this as well as I do. You entreated me so earnestly, with all your heart. Your words cut me to the quick. I sat down on the fence posts stacked up against the sheep shed. I pointed at the mountains around us and, forcing back tears, muttered a verse by Sigurður Breiðfjörð:

> *Motherland, my place of birth,*
> *by every man beloved so true.*
> *Where daylight brought me life and mirth,*
> *where the child I was matured and grew.*

"Don't give me any fucking doggerel about some goddamned motherland," you said. So foul-mouthed and assertive you could be—it made you even more attractive, but made me even less certain about what I should do. You said you couldn't continue living there in eternal shame, under the nose of Hallgrímur and his kin throughout the district. How were you supposed to go to the Co-op like a respectable person? "There she is, the adulteress who let Bjarni knock her up while she was married to Hallgrímur."

I said I would go to the Co-op.

No. No compromises were possible. You weren't going to let any ugly talk of adultery go around and shouldn't have to spend all your time denying rumors, trapped by "the parish's slanderous windpipe." That's how you put it. Damn, you were good at putting things into words, my dearest Helga. I got that expression from you: the parish's slanderous windpipe.

Hallgrímur had been intimate with you as well. If I didn't want you, the child would be his.

I needed to think things over. I walked off across the homefield. It cut me to the quick when you informed me softly that I didn't have much time.

For the next few nights I didn't sleep. I lay there tossing and turning, got up and went to the sheep shed and asked the sheep whether they could imagine having a new master. I was even

considering working for the Americans in Reykjavík. I told the
sheep that I loved a woman. They gave me puzzled looks. I bridled
my Skjóni and rode up the valley. The grass on the gravel banks
swayed in the warm wind and a low cloud bank slung itself over
the peaks and down the scree-covered slopes. I rode the path over
the gravel bed, through the tussocky ground, past a boggy hollow and more grassy banks. I stopped to rest at the hill where the
Viking settler lies and the horses never graze. Looked over the farm
where Grandmother and Grandfather lived; they were so good to
me when I was a child. Grandma Kristín seemed as old as the set-
tlers of this land; in my memory she's bathed in sweet antiquity.
When she grew up there was no soap in the countryside; clothes
and sheets were washed with lant, as had been done since time
immemorial. She said that women today didn't have hair, just dead
tufts on their heads. In her youth, when women washed their hair
with urine, their locks glowed long and thick, as she put it.

Fantastically shaped clouds passed over me in the hollow,
and I always felt as if these forms wanted to tell me something, as
if they had a personal message for me. Would I ever cloud-gaze in
Reykjavík? Wouldn't my senses seem barnacle-grown in relation
to the beauty of life?

Should I move to Reykjavík to dig ditches or put up Quonset-
hut barracks for the Americans? Give up the sheep that my father

had bequeathed me and that I'd worked day and night to refine and increase, resulting in them usually bearing twins or triplets? Leave the district where my forefathers had lived for an entire millennium, to work in a city where one never beholds the product of one's hands and instead becomes a renter and another man's slave? Where people say time is money and spend on the theater and other entertainments what they earn in offices, wearing polyester suits? Away from the hidden people in the mountain slopes. From the places where history speaks from every hill and every hollow. Where I'd shot a fox shitting. Away from the stones that I conversed with as a child. From the cotton-grass moors and the slopes that embody ancient mystery. Why couldn't we two thrive here in this corner of the country? Was I never again to see the luxuriant grass on the Hvaleyrarholt hayfield, which I'd cultivated? There may have been abundance and ample wealth in Reykjavík today, but tomorrow? Who knew?

I remember saying that human societies were like apples. The bigger, the less taste. I knew this from the apples that old Jensi had ordered at the co-op.

You said I knew squat about apples or Reykjavík. You always had an answer for everything. It was something to behold.

I went to visit my father's grave and recalled the promise I gave him when he made me his heir on his deathbed. Kolkustaðir had been in the family for nine generations, and I said I wasn't going to let the farm out of our family's hands. My brother Sigurjón had just died of tuberculosis, my nephew Marteinn was only a child, and my sister Lilja was an invalid. Some damned thing had gotten in her head and she deteriorated steadily. Whatever happened, I knew that my soul would be here, that I couldn't take it with me to Reykjavík.

"Up to you," you said. If that was my choice, I'd just have to live with it!

You turned pink and pursed your lips. Your eyes. I couldn't look into them, it was too painful.

The ties between us seemed to break in a single moment. Or did they?

You knew that it was my child, but no one was ever to find out. From here on, our relationship was finished. Never more, we two. Late one evening by the barn door, and then we were done.

Do you remember what it says in *Grettis saga*? Many a thing can occur at late evening.

I remember that my heart told me I loved you, when I looked at you and saw how serious and determined you were, drying your tears and telling me this, as I stood there like an upended, weather-beaten driftwood log. I just loved you more. Isn't that what happens to a man in the presence of the one he desires most, dear Helga? Doesn't he become a pale driftwood stump and retreat from true love?

Before I knew it, I started watching how your belly grew. From a distance. The old saying proved true, that a fire of love lit by a large flame can never be extinguished in one evening.

Ever since that evening, I've been the one who didn't go, the one who chose a little farm over love. I admit that sometimes it was difficult. Once, for instance, when I visited your farm as Hay Officer to inspect the hay and live-stock, little Hulda came running to me and hopped into my arms. She was about three years old at the time, the poor thing, and knew me only in the way that kin recognizes kin by intu-ition and sense. An all-encompassing feeling of love poured over me. She had white tresses that sparkled in the sun—they were whiter than swans' wings—and asked whether I wanted to play with her in the sandbox. In her pure kid's voice, with wonder in her blue eyes. Then you came out and saw us in the yard; no doubt you remember this. You waved her away. Told her to stop *footling* around with strangers. That was the word you used—footling.

I went off to the sheep shed. Sat down on the pile of hay where we had made love not so long ago, or so it seemed to me; where what seemed like just moments ago, I watched your breasts bob on your rib cage like swans on the waves.

No matter how I tried to bear up, tears forced their way out of me like spots of blood through gauze. My sobs were distorted. I felt my will sink into my legs; they wanted to get up, march to your door, where I should say to you: "Let's go." These words alone. Let's go. But I hardened my resolve. "Up onto the keel." I thought of what kind of person I would become in Reykjavík. Destitute with you and three children. Could I love you—and your children with Hallgrímur—under such circumstances? Is it so certain, Helga, that everything would have been fine for us? I would have dug a ditch for you and filled it back up again, the same ditch all my life. I would have walked miles for you every single day, back and forth, wearing out pairs and pairs of shoes, just hoping to be able to touch you with a single fingertip. I would have eaten soap for you, if you'd asked me to. But to abandon myself, the countryside and farming, which were who I am; that I couldn't do. It was just as well that I pulled myself together. As I was wiping away my tears there in the hay, Hallgrímur appeared in the doorway.

I admit that I sometimes wondered how I might get rid of him and make it look like an accident. That useless excuse for a farmer and lazybones in everything except maybe breaking mares. I thought about asking him to come help me fix the trailer coupler on the Farmall and seeing to it that the tractor kicked into gear—this happened often, by accident—with the throttle set on high, and backed over him before being able to stop. But these were just pitiful imaginings on my part, a kind of pettish consolation forcing its way into my consciousness without my being able to prevent it. I understood that these thoughts sprung from my dissatisfaction with myself, and that such silly ideas were just temporary relief. Of course, I could never have done him any harm. Things weren't supposed to go as they did for my namesake in the novel *Guillemot*. That was never the idea.

I remember it was the same year the atom bombs were dropped on Japan. In the fall we were called together to the meeting house for some reason, and this new peril was quickly on everyone's lips.

Some had heard that enough bombs had been made to destroy all life on earth—more than once. Others said that now all hell could break loose, and no one could do anything about it.

Ingjaldur of Hóll spoke up and, with a profound expression, said that mankind had never built an apparatus that he wasn't able to handle. Then the farmhand from Rauðamelur, his hair slicked with brilliantine, stood up and said he knew an example of such. Héðinn of Klaufnabrekka constructed himself a wheelbarrow far too large, shoveled it full of cow dung, and set off with it down his steep hayfield, but then he couldn't keep it steady and it tipped over the verge. And there it still was.

Following the farmhand's story, the assembly fell silent.

Gunnar of Hjarðarnes broke the silence. "Well, you don't say," he said, before shaking his handkerchief open and blowing his nose. And with that, the list of scheduled speakers was finished. Those who had prepared lines of snuff before the speeches commenced snorting them now, blew their noses, and said "mm-hmm" and "yessir," and soon the meeting came to an end.

10

I invested in another pair of binoculars. Ordered the big book of birds from Reykjavík. My Unnur remarked on how keen I was on bird-watching. I almost never paid attention to the birds, except when Unnur or someone else caught me off guard, or could see me, in which case I would look up the slope or down the valley and say something about how unusual it was for the snipes to lay their eggs so high up in the scree. Or mentioned how the purple sandpipers were gathering early down on the spits, or how little there was for the tern to feed its young this summer. I only paid attention to her. And to you. Watched her swing all by herself on the farmyard swing set that I'd helped you assemble for your older kids, Einar and Vigdís, a long time ago. How she called to you when you hung out the laundry, no doubt asking you to give her a push. Called to Hallgrímur, who shuffled around the farmyard restlessly, completely ignoring her. Saw how she sat in the swing, looking as serious as you did when you bore her in your womb. How she looked down at the grass with dreamy eyes. How she stuck out her tongue when she concentrated on shoveling in the sandbox—which I built for her; how she ran in circles around the homefield. How she stumbled. Cried. Stood up again. Prepared food just like you, serving up sheep bones with sand sauce. From a distance, I watched my daughter making mud pies, until I was overcome with emotion and could no longer see anything through the binoculars because the eye cups were full of tears.

I composed a verse and likened her to sunbeams, how they warm and delight you, yet it's neither possible to catch them in your hands nor claim them for yourself. They're of another world, like her white tresses that fluttered in the sunshine breeze.

My heart is warmed by beams of sun,
as by the tresses white you wore.
Yet both of these I take as one—
my heart and mind both long for more.

You two are the only religion I've ever had. I haven't chosen to kiss up to God and Christ when things have gone badly in my life. There are, of course, many who suffer from hunger and poverty. I've always had enough for me and mine and accepted responsibility for the decisions I've made, not interfering with those distinguished gentlemen in their jobs. I've also understood that this God in Heaven must be at least partly created by man. I guess I know He exists, but He's hardly the type to sport whiskers. I've felt rather that He speaks to mankind in the autumn colors of the crops, or in the scent of newly cut driftwood pieces that cleave so exquisitely into fence posts and outlast their maker.

I've had ideals and lost them. Perhaps my belief in the Association of Icelandic Cooperative Societies was a kind of religion to begin with. I sat for a long time on the board of the Co-op and oversaw the slaughtering and salting for the Norwegian market. They used to say that three knives could be seen in the air when I chined lambs' spines, butchering them into large cuts to go into oaken barrels, in much the same way that three swords were seen aloft when Gunnar from Hlíðarendi brandished his blade. The Association was originally an organization of farmers formed to protect their own interests and ensure a good price for their product. This was, might I say, the only sign of socialism that I've ever seen in these parts, and probably the only example of socialism in this whole country before or since; some farmers had so much ardent faith in the ideal that never an unkind word could be spoken of the Association. Now I've witnessed the decline of both the Co-op and sheep farming, because that ideal was forgotten along the way, as well as the farmers; the Association turned into an empire and freeloader's club in Reykjavík, driving a wedge into the cooperative ideal. They've come a long way toward eliminating all sheep farming in this country; that's what came of the ideal, and what the skald declared is right: "The first to light the fires seldom enjoy their warmth."

You know, Helga, I'm not your typical old coot who praises the past and finds fault with everything contemporary. We know that progress has been made in many areas. Do you suppose that any other generation will experience such drastic changes in its circumstances in one lifetime? We who grew up in a culture that had experienced little change since the time of the settlement and who also got to know the dubious modern world: its technology and its pasteurized milk products. Of course it was an

improvement when rubber boots arrived. I wasn't yet of confir-
mation age when my father sent me up the valley to the moorland to mow, and there I stood half the summer with moor slop
squishing in my sheepskin shoes, finally leaving me seriously ill
with pleurisy. I was only allowed to rest a few days before he
sent me back up the valley. It took many years to regain my full
strength, and I declare to you that such a person is extremely
relieved when his first pair of boots is handed to him. Yet we
watched the old turf farmhouses of Hörgár Parish being cleared
away by bulldozers upon the arrival of cement. It's one thing to
believe in and devote oneself to progress, Helga, and another to
start despising the old ways. The old turf farms are all gone now
because they reminded people of cold and damp and what people
so mercilessly call "hayseedism." But what culture do people have
who say such things? It's only when folk turn their backs on their
own history that they become small. And it was no small revolu-
tion when the telephone and television came to the countryside.
Grandma Kristín asked how they fit a whole person into such
a little box, meaning the radio. But another thing she said was
truer, that everything spoken on the telephone was a lie, and
because of that it couldn't be trusted. And though one might glo-
rify the radio receiver and the usefulness of the weather reports,
the fact is that one remembers little or nothing of what comes out

of it. On the other hand, family readings of the *Passion Hymns* or *Vídalín's Sermons* are as if engraved in my memory: the expressions on the reader's face, the clarity of his voice, the sighs as he read, and the discussion afterward. And wasn't it true what old Vídalín said, that it's easy for evil to keep good in check, but difficult for good to keep evil in check. The radio came, and Vídalín died—as Bárður of Staður declared in his poem.

What one really remembers best is when people gather together, for instance out in front of the Co-op, or for the Reading Club, and the storytelling spirit takes flight. People these days don't talk to each other; they don't gather anymore! Good storytellers are nowhere to be found.

I've tried to do more than just farming and fishing. I fought for various causes that I felt were important. I took on the task of building fifteen-thread jenny wheels for several homes, because there was no reason for people in the countryside to be sitting around doing nothing in the winter while it was possible to multiply the value of the wool fivefold.

I did a great deal of handwork. Made button holders of bone and horsehair and lamp brushes and brooms from the same material, rope buckles for pack saddles, ash cans from sheets of tin, clothespins of wood. I built tables and chairs for the kitchen and the other rooms, and for the chairs, Unnur embroidered exceptionally elegant cushions that turned out to be very popular. I made washtubs and watering troughs, buckets, cabinets, created lampshades from wolffish and spotted wolffish skin, and built a trunk that I covered with sealskin, just as the late Gísli Konráðsson did. The list could go on. It's a damned culture shock to see how homes look these days, when every single thing is from its own part of the world, and very often people have no idea where those things come from. What separates something homemade from something factory-produced? One has a soul and the other doesn't, because whoever makes something with his own hands leaves behind a piece of himself in his work. I wrote an article for *The Farmer's Journal* in which I asked why the only models and patterns for sewing were found in foreign fashion magazines. Why were Icelandic women imitating foreign forms, but then couldn't learn Icelandic handicrafts anywhere— brocading in the old style, lace knitting, crocheting, bobbin lace-making, or embroidering with gold and silver thread? What I wrote wasn't really very remarkable. And afterward I saw that I was perhaps trying to justify life here in the countryside in the face of all those stylish fashion magazines that you said were in Reykjavík. But I'm not going to change my opinion. If people had continued to develop and promote Icelandic handicrafts and the domestic wool industry, more culture would be found in contemporary Icelandic homes, not just piles of mass-produced items, each more soulless than the next.

At the post-roundup dance in the autumn, Ingjaldur of Hóll came to speak to me and said that he'd heard I was having a hard time giving Unnur a child. Word had started going around the district that Unnur couldn't have children. I'm sure this wasn't meant badly, but when he started talking about pinching her back firmly, or putting ice cubes on her nether regions, I turned and walked out.

11

I t was in the spring, when I let out the lambs, that it hit me hardest, the desire that you abandon your pride and come over to me. And always when the dandelions started spreading over the fields, yellow flames kindled in another place as well. I would have left Unnur, yet seen to it that she lacked nothing. But you always stuck to your cursed pride, as did all your kin from Breiðafjörður, where, long ago, Guðrún's cheeks turned scarlet and she married Bolli out of sheer pride.

Bloody cursed pride.

Forgive me.

I'm sorry, Helga.

I got a bit worked up. It's all right. Naturally, when I view things objectively, I'm unable to see which was worse: my stubbornness in staying on the farm or your pride. It's certain that neither would yield. I know it would have been difficult for you to live here with me. On the next farm over. Side by side with Hallgrímur. But I also know that I would have wasted away in Reykjavík, that my will to live would have ebbed. When things became difficult between us, I would have always longed to be back in the countryside. You would have sensed it. Who knows what would have happened.

But my desire for you burned in my flesh. It made me shudder sometimes. Once in late April I woke up standing out in the hayfield, wearing only my long underwear and sporting an erection! Thank God it was early morning, and no one witnessed it as far as I know. I'd been sleepwalking. I'd dreamed of you. I dreamed that I'd sold the farm for thirty hens—not silver—and was on my way to your place with the hens in a cage to tell you that now we should set off for Reykjavík. But first you wanted to make love with me, and had taken off all your clothes in the barn. You can imagine how pathetic I felt when the dream ended. A person standing in a hayfield in Iceland in the dead of night, wearing only his tattered underwear, his dick sticking out like a stranded sperm whale; someone who has chosen toiling in the countryside over love. "Woman is sometimes my grief," declared Björn the Champion of Breiðavík; "a bright and pure maiden loves me," declared another; and a third said that souls who love will never be parted. Do you know which of these applies to us? I don't.

I never went behind your back to try to get to Hulda. We'd made an agreement. I arrived last at church and sat nearest the door, while you sat up front with your folk. You quit the Women's Club, and I always let you know a day ahead whenever I came to inspect the hay and examine the animals, so that you could keep Hulda away. We worked together to keep it secret, as cooperative as we were during haymaking. Concealing what was true and right.

Covering up our true sparks, ignited by Mother Nature.

Hadn't it gone far enough, Helga?

Once Hulda and a friend of hers rode horses over to my farm. She was about fifteen or sixteen, had come to stay in the countryside with her "daddy" during a school holiday, and the girls had stolen away and drunk a bit of moonshine. They were so lively and jovial here in the kitchen that my house felt like a tomb a long time afterward. Hulda said she was starting high school, and her friend related that Hulda had received the highest marks of all. I mixed a little cocktail of vodka and ginger ale and poured each of them a glass. Unnur was scandalized and went up to her room. They said that there were endless parties and rock and roll in Reykjavík. They both joked and laughed and asked whether I knew how to jive or if I'd heard of rock and roll. I enjoyed their exuberance immensely.

But suddenly everything in me went black. I thought I would pass out, asked them to excuse me, and hurried out to the barn. As soon as I'd shed my tears there in the barn, my anger flared. I found existence to be unjust and my life devoid of all meaning. I was angry at you for sparking this life with me and then taking it away, and now it looked as if this life had come only to mock me and reveal to me my destitution.

I didn't feel better when I returned to the kitchen and Hulda asked why Unnur and I didn't have any children. I declare to you, Helga, that this was also hard for me; at least you gained the fruit of our passion. I: nothing. And after Hulda became a television announcer, thereby entering people's homes every single evening to read the schedule, it didn't do anything to help me forget or relieve the tightness around my heart. Quite the contrary. I tried to read in her facial expressions, in her voice, whether she was happy, whether she was well-married there in Reykjavík, whether she wasn't simply thankful for having been created. She was so beautiful. Sometimes, when Unnur wasn't sitting in her chair, I went up to the screen and touched Hulda's face and hair.

I can tell you a story that took place many years ago. One evening we were both sitting in the living room, Unnur knitting in her chair. Hulda had just announced the evening's schedule, when I stood up and yanked the television free from the wall; I threw it straight out the living-room window, causing a frightful explosion in the yard as the screen shattered. Outside, the dog barked, baffled as to what was going on. Unnur paled and stopped knitting. She looked at the footstool where the television had previously stood, as if her soul couldn't comprehend its sudden disappearance.

I said, "There's never anything on this damned TV."

She said, "Why didn't you throw it out the door instead?"

12

I could accept living in town if so many people didn't become so boring living there. Even the ducks on the Pond, who get as much to eat as they want, lose their radiance, their personalities. When the Co-op sent me to Reykjavík, and I wandered down to the Pond, I saw that the birds behaved differently there. They weren't curious or playful, like birds in the wild. The ducks at the Pond had become just like the people: dull parasites who quarrel over what's thrown to them.

Isn't it precisely this that makes you think life has no purpose? Precisely among the creatures that have lost the connection with their true nature? I could have become either a street sweeper or gas-station attendant; when I died no one would have paid any attention. I would simply have been replaced. I would have become a laborer in Reykjavík, and a dull glow would have reflected from my being.

I've lived all my days with the rediscovery of love as my embers of hope. Those embers would have died out in a few months in Reykjavík. I would have found my work empty of meaning, felt boredom wash over me, and started drinking to entertain myself. That's how they turn out in Reykjavík. I see it from the movies they make about folk in the countryside: they're portrayed as poorly indoctrinated numbskulls who occupy themselves only by being horrid to their next of kin, expressing themselves in one-syllable words. So I see what they're up to in Reykjavík, those miserable people there. Do you think that I could have loved you in such a place, Helga? And if we accept what people in modern cities believe, that happiness consists of being able to buy so much from shops that one becomes destitute inside, that happiness is being free to choose whatever one pleases in life, as if the world were one universal restaurant, isn't that a judgment against all past generations that weren't able to live so? Aren't happiness and fulfillment in life, then, brand-new inventions of city people, while all past life in this country, in fact, the lion's share of all life, of all times, is both meaningless and hapless? I'm not certain that the bright gleam in the eyes of my grandmother, Kristín, and her cheerful mood harmonize with such a view of history.

Damn this capitalist lie! "Curse that hag," I say, as Grettir said of the old woman. It's precisely these types of people, who never questioned the values and standards of their time, that became Nazis down south in Germany. Sometimes it seems that humans can be impressed with any sort of rubbish imaginable, so gullible and helpless they are.

I would have taken desperate measures to overcome the tedium and emptiness that comes with choosing everything as if off a menu. Was I supposed to build barracks and dig ditches for the Americans? Those soulless creatures! They could all take themselves off to the moon as far as I was concerned—and stay there. Was I supposed to work for them and thereby become like them?

Could I have loved you then?

I don't regret anything, Helga. You wanted to have it this way. I maintain that, in fact, I never had any choice.

The choice was yours.

And you didn't want me.

13

Every single day of my life I've taken delight in my animals. I've saved many a man who had mechanical trouble, because I learned a lot about farm equipment in the Agricultural College's classes and by my own effort, and I knew how to work a lathe and was fond of iron, as was said of Skallagrímur. I've given people lustrous fresh fish to eat and always had a barrel of salted seal-pup blubber on hand, to the great delight of anyone who dropped in. My smoked lump-sucker was known throughout the country, and I received many a word of thanks for it. I've bred and improved my sheep stock, which Marteinn, my brother Bjössi's son, obviously appreciates. I've rescued a drowning man and found another one lost up on a heath in a driving snowstorm. I've taken shits in snowstorms. Wiped my ass with snow. I've waded out to skerries after children and lambs. I sat for a long time on the parish council and the board of the Co-op and made improvements in the butchering process, which I also supervised for the Co-op. I took an active part in the Reading Group of Hörgár Parish and handled its book purchases for a long period of time. I recall the days when farmers thought for themselves and disagreed with the existential philosophy from more southern climes, that claimed life was futile, like a man rolling a rock up a mountainside only to chase it back down again before starting all over.

"That's utter bullshit," said old Gísli of Lækur. It simply wasn't like that. It's more like the nature of man for him to roll a rock up a mountainside in order to prop it up there on top and then stack stones around it to make a handsome cairn. Man wished to build memorials to his own work. Another philosopher we read in Danish translation says that man's existential dilemma consists of having to choose everything in this world, which is the root of his unhappiness. I remember Jósteinn asking in his quiet, hoarse voice, reminding one of a distant cry from a heath, if mankind was supposed to spend a long time each morning pondering whether he should have bread or stones for breakfast?

"No, listen, mate," said Gunnar of Hjarðarnes. He'd heard that this man sat all day in cafés in a big city with the menu before him and used his café existence as the basis for his theories on the lives of all men. That life is about choosing everything as if off a menu. Our discussion continued in this vein. These were people who had come up with their own meaning of life. They were instinctively clever, because no school had told them how to think. They thought for themselves. Such people are gone now, and I scarcely believe they raise them in Reykjavík nowadays.

Here, in the countryside, I've been important. And if I haven't been important, at least I've felt I was important. There's a huge difference. Here, I've beheld the product of my hands. I hadn't yet turned fifty when I went to meet old Jón Eysteinsson, the director of the Agricultural Bank, and paid off all my loans.

Don't city dwellers complain about not belonging to the world, about being emotionless and dull, and then seek gratification in drugs and extramarital affairs? And then their only question is whether they should kill themselves or not. Or else wait a while. Is there anything more horrible than waiting for life to pass by? Instead of getting down to business and bringing home the bacon. And then they compose poems and write stories about the loneliness and cold of the city. Why did they leave the countryside, after all? Who asked them to do so? If all life is fiction, as they say, isn't there more growth and goodness in the hayfields, more luster and a fresher feeling of freedom in the air here? You know, Helga, I've heard that old Greek and Roman poets, as well as great philosophers and sages around the world, liken life to a dream, to fiction. But a bird in the hand is worth two in the bush. You can find the same wisdom simply by turning to my grandmother, who knows neither how to read nor write, but can recite a poem composed by an unknown poet and never considered good enough to write down:

> *Life is reverie and dream,*
> *calm day, breaking sea and so,*
> *skerry and strong stream,*
> *storm, fog, and powdery snow.*
> *Blossom and sunbeams, we mustn't forget.*
> *But behind the mountains heaven-high –*
> *none has caught sight yet.*

I'm not saying that everything is so heavenly here and the people are utter angels. Of course there's rumormongering and jealousy

and all sorts of other hogwash. But these same people loan you
a tractor tire in a pinch. Even Ingjaldur from Hóll—he helped
me out when I needed it. He respected me, even though we had
differences of opinion. And when he said that about pinching
Unnur's back, I knew that this was done with cows that were
difficult to impregnate, and it was the only way he could think of
dealing with such a dilemma. He didn't mean it badly; I saw in
his eyes that he wished me well, the dear man.

I've learned to read the snort in the bull's nostrils. Have felt
the natural will of my livestock encompass and invigorate me.
I've seen the blue-clad elf and heard fetches knock on the door.
Felt the secret powers of existence in hills and enchanted spots,
and shooed off the guardian spirits of the land when my horse
balked. Saw the light long ago. No one understands that it's possible to see the light long ago, but it's all the same to me if no one
understands what is meant. I've learned to read the clouds and
birds and the behavior of a dog. Perceived the wonder of the settlement of this country and felt the magnificence of its original
inhabitants. I've sensed the anguish of the leaves in a lunar eclipse
and gazed up the slopes feeling my soul lifted from me as I drove
the Farmall. I've heard my stomach grumble back at the thunder,
a little man beneath a big sky; heard the stream whisper that it's
eternal. Made the earth my beloved. Held a powerful salmon.

Let the fox teach me what it is to be clever. I've felt sympathy looking in a seal's eyes when I had it in my sights, and spared it. Witnessed both the ferocity of the killer whale and the gentleness of motherly love, and found a place of refuge from the world where the swans sleep. Bathed myself in water pregnant with glistening sun, not in murky pipe water used by civilization, and noticed a distinct difference between the two. I've lost my way in a blinding snowstorm leading a horse up a mountain slope and given up, letting the horse's instinct bring me safely home. Shot a fox shitting. Seen an iceberg overturn. Thrown a lumpsucker at the parish council chairman's head. Forgotten a corpse. Fetched a smoked woman. Lived on promise alone during the harsh winters of the early sixties, written things in the lacunae of existence, and understood that a man can dream big dreams on small pillows. I've kept going, intoxicated with desire and the hope that drives sap into the withered branches of creation. And I have loved, and even been a happy creature for a time.

I've seen my progeny grow and mature before my eyes, and I've wept and thought of you until my flesh burned. Cried out in the heather scent of late summer. Satisfied my urges. Then wept some more. I've seen ravens congregate. Seen mankind naked and forlorn. And felt sorry for it.

Yes. Perhaps I have lived with love, not against it. Love is not just a bourgeois romantic notion of finding the one true match who will fill one's soul so full that it brims over and splashes out uninterruptedly as if from some eternal pump. Love is also in this life that I've lived here in the countryside. And when I chose this life and pursued it and didn't regret it, I learned that one should stick to one's decision, nurture it and not deviate—that this is an expression of love. Here beneath the slope of Ljósuvöll is where I had to be. I had no choice.

The choice was yours.

The choice is yours. And I am yours.

Still.

When you became pregnant and asked me to accompany you to Reykjavík, I came to a crossroads in my life. The path that I'd followed up until then branched. I took both paths. Yet neither of them rightly, in the sense that I followed one of them—but had all my heart on the other. With you.

14

Have I mentioned man's depravity, Helga? I no longer believe in the beautiful teachings, and least of all do I intend to preach them here, on the banks of my grave, in this letter to you. We might devote a few words to the subject, the little that this farmer believes he's discovered about human nature in the nearly ninety years that he's lingered here—namely, that deep in each man's heart dwells a depravity, described excellently by old Paul the Apostle in the Bible, that the good that I will, I do not; but the evil that I hate, I do.

One can say fair things about love, dear Helga, but it's usually a bad sign, because it means one's on the brink of opposing it openly. I've seen this in a lot of people. They create beautiful poems about love or deliver speeches about it at fine gatherings, but as they vanish back into their daily routines, it's as if they strip themselves of the trappings of the elegant words and linger loveless the better part of their lives. That's how it looks to me, the phenomenon itself—man, and me myself, quite frankly. It's as if man's desires are never pure and in harmony with the beauty that life has tried to indoctrinate in him. Damned if man doesn't keep trying to arrange his life completely contrary to the good that he knows is deep inside him! I'm not saying that man does his best to be an unmitigated villain—but perhaps he never makes a decent try for the opposite either. There's a huge gap between the two, and in that gap is the field where most people hatch into existence, bloom, and wither away. How did it go, that verse of Kristján Ólason?

> Deep down inside my heart there lay
> —same as others gained indeed—
> a clew to point to me the way,
> though I to it paid little heed.

So, the rule appears to me rather to be that people usually live at odds with what they preach, whatever form that might take, be it a political agenda or, say, existential philosophy. It's as if those who talk about dieting always put the most sugar on their pancakes and the worst louts talk about "care taken for human souls"; those who condemn the crime the loudest are generally the biggest criminals; capitalism, which is supposed to make everyone rich, makes everyone poor; and you can bet that freedom, which people talk so much about now, will eventually make everyone slaves.

Once for the Reading Club I ordered a book about Christopher Columbus and America; the book gave an account of his personal diary entries in which he describes the Indians that he discovered on the shores of the Americas. The Indians went about buck-naked and had an abundance of everything, their children made toys of gold nuggets, and they were given to great warmth and kindness. Isn't such an existence the goal of our civilization? Or have I misunderstood the gist of the grand speeches? Later, after I ordered Halldór Laxness's translation of Voltaire's *Candide*, I saw that the dreamland represented in El Dorado—the most splendid goal of our civilization—is precisely like this little community that Columbus encountered and described two hundred years earlier. On the other hand, what Columbus did to this little dream society that he himself called Paradise is an excellent exemplum on human behavior. After encumbering the islanders, eating and drinking their stores without contributing anything themselves, Columbus and his companions had to flee from their growing and justifiable resentment. Several years later, Columbus returned with armed men, asking the children to show him where they found the gold nuggets they played with; thereafter, they sentenced the whole lot, naked and defenseless, to slave labor, digging gold for him. Isn't this an excellent allegory for man's behavior in regard to Paradise—the dreamland and love, which they never grow tired of chewing over, whether in church or at secular gatherings?

Don't you see the double standard in this, Helga? In all that they say, and on the other hand do. They say: to live is to love. Such is their mantra, but in life itself, they linger in fear and anxiety and dare not go anywhere near love. And if they do venture near it, before they realize it they've sold it cheaper than Judas sold Christ. Cowards and laggards, all of them, and I declare to you that I am the lowest of them all.

Wouldn't it be wise, now that I've started scribbling these lines to you, dear Helga, for me to devote a few words to the low and contemptible in this farmer, to his depravity, as it might be called? This depravity never fails to shock me when I grasp for it in candid moments. Why, for goodness' sake, does a man desire a woman other than his own all his life, yet never takes a single step toward attaining the object of his desire? You see what a Christian life I've lived, my dear; of course one mustn't covet one's neighbor's wife. But it strikes me that I've loved you, Helga—I never grow tired of speaking your name aloud and writing it: Helga…it kisses my palate before it opens my mouth as wide as it can—that I've loved you only to live in anguish and an intentional lovelessness. That the distance from you kindled a longing for closeness, but as soon as that closeness was offered, I withdrew and would sacrifice nothing!

I haven't been able to decipher the mystery of this behavior, and that for the only type of creature to consider itself sensible! I declare it straight from the heart, Helga: I've become like a worm-riddled log, lying here utterly rotten on the shores of time, where the surf will soon take me and no one will shed a tear when I'm gone. Yes, it's true what the ancients said: "With age comes cowardice."

15

was saying that I astonished myself. I don't know any longer whether my desire for you has anything to do with you at all, or whether it hints only at my sick inclination toward masochism. Were you perhaps the innocent object of this depravity of mine, which lies as if hidden in fissures deeper than the rays of language can reach? I know that others took a shine to you as well—I could see how they drank in your form whenever you walked out of the Co-op. No one can ever tell me that you weren't the most handsome woman in this parish.

And since I'm lancing my boils in this letter of mine, you can probably guess that my longing for you wasn't entirely confined to my mind. It was a reality in this hapless farmer's body for many years after things ended between us; the flames couldn't be quenched in one late evening. If only you could have just gone and not appeared before my eyes every single day in my binoculars! It would have made it easier to forget you.

It was the autumn after little Hulda jumped into my arms.

The lambs were down from the mountain and either at the slaughterhouse or in the sheep shed for their winter sojourn. I was checking the smoothness of a yearling ewe's rib tips and found no flaws when you and our little private joke about touching the female kind and assessing her contours crossed my mind. I held it by the neck with one hand as I felt its legs, its rump quite thick and filled out down to the hocks; then I ran my fingers along the ribs and thence to the loin and you haunted my thoughts. I started seeing you in place of that damned ewe lamb and felt as if you were near me again, hearing your voice so tender inside me, how you moaned and trembled as I checked the curvature of your breast in the light from the cracks in the equipment shed's walls, the air pungent with the fragrance of glycerol and grease; so graceful were your curves, I felt as if my palms were filled to bursting with your supple tussocks, and the curls in the coarse wool reminded me of your triangular tuft, and damned if I didn't catch a whiff of the aroma that enveloped my memory of our first union and I simply had to feel you encompassing me, had to have you and hear you moan with lustful ecstasy just one more time, inhale your aroma for the final time…

I sank down to the grating and lay there a considerable while. With my ass crack bare and glaring like a pansy in an old slanderous verse. I'm not certain how long I lay there, defeated by my own depravity and devoid of all decency, but I do know that as soon as I'd hitched up my trousers my first task was to slaughter the ewe. I tossed her into a sack, hauled it up into the dory, and sailed far out beyond the reef, where I tied two large sinkers to it and sank it altogether.

The spot where I sank her was not chosen randomly. It was on the fishing bank where your silo could be seen against the waterfall, the tower that carried the echo of when we made love. I let the boat drift for a long time and stared at the bright red blood oozing from the corpse. Little waves rocked; there was a chilly but gentle southeasterly breeze. Now I'll just let myself go as well, I thought, and completely free of any internal struggle or hesitation, I grabbed the gunwales with both hands.

Cast myself over the side and into the sea.

Panic seized me when I felt the shock of the cold sea and I—or, better put, my voice—started crying out that I couldn't do this. Perhaps it's not enough for a person, alone and loveless, to imagine that no one would care if he killed himself; it's as if the will to live were in the body, and the body seemed not to heed such decisions of the mind. On the other hand, I should mention that I still came close to dying, because I was so paralyzed with cold that I thought I could never get back up in the boat again.

I finally managed to tie a loop from a tattered piece of cord that hung, by coincidence, over the gunwale; I got my knee in the loop, set the cord on the spool, and managed to kick myself up. My life literally hung by a rotten old thread. I wriggled aboard and collapsed in the prow, where I lay for a long time, exhausted. I listened to the wind and rocked in the waves and felt peculiarly well, as if I had managed to erase the outlines of sorrow from my breast for one earthly moment. Then I woke to the spouting of a pod of porpoises swimming by.

I was grateful to be alive; I knew that I should be humble and thankful for what life had handed me. I got to my feet and started punching myself to warm up, before hearing at the corner of my senses a clear and pure female voice coming as if from the reef, so pure that my heart skipped a beat. The voice shouted: "Welcome back!"

There was no one to witness it but me. It's at such moments, dear Helga, which doubtless sound so peculiar described to others, that one understands life is larger than one can comprehend—it was as if life itself were calling! Just take this as the senile chatter of a bedridden old man, Helga, I don't mind; but how precious are such moments—and I'm convinced that others experience sacred moments, which don't become any clearer when one attempts to sort them out.

Despite the fortunate ending to this nonsense, I, Bjarni Gíslason of Kolkustaðir, was as helpless and forlorn a person as before. Someone who lived with the fact that love and the fullness of existence were things that belonged to "the other side," as Unnur always called your farm; and though I began to despise my lust after this, and had long stopped quenching it in summertime dips in the spring, nature would not be mocked and instead sought an outlet in sleep. If I weren't wandering out to the hayfield with my erection sticking out—did I mention that?—I would wake wet and sticky beneath my long underwear after having banged you in some dream—usually after having rubbed and felt out your whole body with the lant in the good old portable bathtub. I declare, as it says in the hymn: Man, who shall bear your heavy load?

16

Following this failed attempt at disposing of myself came a period in my life that I find impossible to see clearly under the searchlights of my consciousness. I wonder if I even existed. Observed closely, I would have turned out to be just a person in trousers, rubber boots, and a belt buckle tinted with verdigris; a person who tended his livestock and fulfilled his obligations. But inside me, the spark of life was extinguished. I remember that I tried to be thankful for what I had, but there was a hollow ring to such thoughts. The passion

that previously kept me afloat day and night was now a fetter
that I began to despise, because I realized that it would never be
quenched. Unnur had to goad me into getting out of bed in the
mornings; the house was empty and bleak; there were no other
people in my life during this period.

Damned if the whole caboodle isn't black and white in
my consciousness, just like the photos from that time. When I
look over this period, I think that it might be best of all never
to encounter love—because after it's lost, you're much worse off
than before. Yes, I've lived what the old folk song says, and maybe
you have too:

> *Love is most passionate*
> *When it's still unachieved.*
> *Never love—you're never bereaved.*

Everything rang hollow; all poetry and song was like hammering
on an empty barrel. A succulent story served up by Gunnar of
Hjarðarnes or one of the other master storytellers failed to touch
me; it rolled off me, like water off a goose, not sticking in my
mind. I suddenly came to my senses out in front of the Co-op,
where everyone was laughing at the story, but it was too late. It
was all too late—past and gone. The voice of my wrung-out soul

had no words. Yet worst of all wasn't feeling the pain or, how shall I put it, feeling nothing, but rather the loneliness in it. No one seemed to pay my infirmity any heed, and no one came to talk to me. Not even Unnur. Nor did it suit me to start bewailing my heartache to her. Yet the worst thing about the deepest pain is how visible it can be to everyone but the person suffering it.

What kept me going were the animals, I do declare, my dear, and no one is alone who has made Icelandic sheep his personal friends—whatever that might mean. There's a radiance in the animals' vitality that relieves pain and allows one to survive every sort of disaster.

This reminds me of the story of Ólöf of the Úteyjar Islands and her hired hands, an older man and a girl who spent the winters with Ólöf out where everything was deserted long before our day. But the memory of the people survives. As winter drew to a close, Ólöf's help started to grow weary of the monotony of sheep tending and wool dressing. Folk say that the lack of tobacco was hard on the man, whereas for the girl, it was the lack of men; so they came up with the idea of secretly breaking various farm implements, such as shovels and rakes, and announcing that they would take them to the mainland for repairs. Ólöf didn't find this sufficient excuse and made the repairs herself, as best she could. Finally the two resorted to extinguishing the fire when Ólöf wasn't there to see it. Returning to the mainland then became a necessity, and the pair rowed to land on Ash Wednesday to satisfy their urges in civilization. That night there was a north wind and severe frost, covering the bay with ice and making it impossible for anyone to reach Ólöf on her island for six weeks. And there she remained, with broken tools, without light and heat, in the cold north wind and darkness. When people finally broke through to the islands, Ólöf was still of sound mind and had managed to keep all of her animals alive. She'd apparently started seeing phantoms and specters in the darkness, the original Viking settler Þórsteinn haunting her the most. The fact is that this great feat of Ólöf of Úteyjar is impossible to comprehend but for the animals—it was the animals that kept her alive, fireless, and not the other way around. And that's how it was with me as well, after you shook me off.

Until it came, the glorious news. You and Hallgrímur were divorcing.

17

Whether I've exaggerated the memory or not, two things are inseparable in my mind: the news of your divorce from Hallgrímur and the virulent breakup of the ice that spring. Of course, old hopes kindled unbridled within me. I thought, like Garún in the story, that it was all for my sake. I decided you would move with your children to Reykjavík, and then everything would be prepared for us to blaze anew. I could take on additional board work for the Association, could perhaps find something to do in the city—part-time work—and hire someone to help Unnur with the farm work in the meantime, staying for longer periods in Reykjavík, not far from you and the children. I'd give you a hand and get a chance to spend time with Hulda; yes, it was a message, deep and quiet like a whisper from the gods, that you could now let go of your pride, give in, because you, as much as I, didn't want everything between us to be shut and locked; perhaps when it came down to it, you had warm feelings toward me. I felt myself released from the spell of gloom, and when in my binoculars, dear Helga, I spied your things being stacked in the farmyard that summer, I thought in my heart—because, like men of old, I have always thought with my heart and not with my head—I thought that now you would only have to wait for a moment; soon I would come to you.

They oughtn't be repeated here, those low and primitive thoughts that the meltwater carried out into the current. You, naked in my mind, and the aroma of stale urine in my nose; I feeling the fullness of your breasts in a fine house in Reykjavík and then the two of us drinking cocoa afterward. Good heavens, God help me, so paltry I am.

Perhaps you understand better now why things happened as they did that September day when I knocked on your door there in the newly built apartment block in the Kampur neighborhood. You opened the door, and outside it stood a man alienated from reality, looking at you. Love had deprived me of all reason as I stood there at the door in my finest clothing, my hair slicked with brilliantine, smelling of newly purchased cologne; I handed you the bouquet and said that I'd come to bring you flowers.

You look as if you've seen a ghost. You stare at me wide-eyed, with your fair cow eyes, which is my personal name for them. You snatch the flowers from my hands and rip them apart and call me an ass and a wretch who should screw off, and then a man comes to the door and shouts: "What person is this?"

And now I shall speak plainly, Helga: at that moment, I felt the life taken from me; I saw only black. I don't remember clearly which of us started it, but I was like an injured and helpless beast, penned in a corner by butchers. My only way out was to bare my teeth or die, so I grabbed the man forcefully and threw him against the wall, despite his being much larger than I, and let the blows rain down on him as you screamed and hit me in the head with the torn bouquet, and your children came to the door and people came out of their apartments into the hallway, but I felt good about it, damn, it was good when you pounded me, this touch was so much better than no touch at all and to me it was sheer bliss to hear you cry again and shout at me, just as you did by the dung-channel of old; you—life—shouting at a block of driftwood. Me.

Then I left.

And truth to tell, I really didn't give a damn where I went.

18

Afterward, my situation grew worse than ever. The queen was gone from my life, replaced by a king named Bacchus. The fact is that I don't have many memories of that winter, and neither before nor after have I behaved in such a contemptible manner. I suppose I did this because I didn't have it in me to kill myself. I brought eternal shame upon myself here in the district, and make no secret of the fact that all the rancor I caused cut me to the core. But good people in the community were kind to me, and this kindness kept me

afloat, Helga—that and the animals. Blessed be human kindness. Just as I have chosen not to focus on the rain but rather
the shine as I scribble these words to you, I'll write no more
concerning that time of degradation and mention instead how
I recovered.

When your letter arrived.

God alone knows how many times I've picked up this letter
and read it. You should see how worn it is. It's as worn as it is holy
to me. I learned every word of it by heart ages ago; I've laid it on
my breast beneath my shirt and wept and sought comfort and
strength in this letter of yours nearly my entire life, or so it seems
to me; but it wasn't until just now, here on the banks of my grave,
that I finally sat down and replied to it, dear Helga. I've never
before felt I needed to answer you; it was enough for me to know
that you'd left Hallgrímur, that you wanted me to come to you,
that you asked me to forgive you. That you said—that you wrote
in your letter—that you—loved me.

This knowledge of warmth on the other side, knowledge that
there was a place where someone thought warmly of me, and
loved me, was more than enough for this farmer. After all that
had happened, and after I came to realize that I would never do
anything else than swim with the tide, I started wishing that you
would find a new man, a good man, who would love you and give

you everything that you could ask for. As far as I know, that man finally came into your life. Yes, in the end I fled when I had the chance. Look, Helga—see what a small person I am, now that the tub has finally been emptied.

I keep one clear childhood memory in my heart, and, in conclusion, I wish to share it with you here. I was only seven, eight years old. My eyes wandered to our homefield and I noticed a gray-brown creature I didn't recognize, so I ran over to it to take a better look. As I drew near, I saw it was a great big eagle that had landed there in the field. It was sickly—mottled gray and patchy—and so feeble that I was able to come quite near it. Its yellow feet and black claws, thick and powerful, witnessed to the ancient grandeur and strength of the old champion. I don't know whether it was simply too old and worn from life's rigors, or was ill from eating the poisoned carrion that was baited for foxes and scavenger birds to keep their numbers in check and protect the breeding grounds of the eider ducks, a bad practice abandoned shortly thereafter. There it had landed, and took it very badly indeed when the young boy came too near. At first it hissed, then screeched and glowered at me, spreading its ragged wings. I saw how tattered it was; many of its flight feathers were missing and its wing bones showed through bare patches, as if its plumage had been plucked off here and there. I thought for certain that this big bird would never fly again and felt sorry for it. I wanted to take it and bring it home with me, but it hopped away and flapped its wings up and down as I ran around the field after it. Its remaining flight feathers whistled and sang with a whining, sucking sound like that of a bilge pump, but then a most astonishing thing happened that shouldn't have: the bird took flight, just barely making it over the fence, and headed straight toward the beach and onward out over the ocean, vanishing from my sight far away where the blue of sea and sky met.

I never saw it again, and the thought has crossed my mind that this vision perhaps wasn't real but rather a dream that became a reality in my mind, a dream with an important message. In fact, I sometimes feel as if my spirit has, just like this bird, tried to fly away from the everyday bustle of earthly life, that I've tried in the same way to glide through the poetic sky with my ragged writing, and if the gods allow it I will doubtless fly precisely in this way to you in the end—on ragged wings.

I find it good and right to have written this letter, dear Helga. And though you're dead and can't read it, I've found it reassuring to scribble these lines to you.

Yesterday, I took my cane and went out for a walk on my decrepit legs and lay down in the grass between the Helga Tussocks as I had so often before. There were cumulus clouds to the south, swiftly moving, but light in the gaps between the cloud banks, and then an absolutely splendid sunbeam shone down between the piles onto me and everything around me—or should I say, rather, onto us—as I lay there on your breasts.

Then the blessed wagtail came and alighted on a nearby tussock, and I asked it, as Grandma Kristín had taught me, where I would live next year. But the wagtail just stood there and wagged its tail up and down, and I knew that the questioner's death was finally ordained. The sunbeam flooded the slope with such light that I felt it to be a beckoning to me from the great spirit behind life, and I started to cry, senile old man that I am, stranded between two tussocks in Iceland, the Helga Tussocks; and I realized that what really hurts in life aren't the sharp points that stab and injure you, but rather the soft call of love that you disregard—the letter from Helga, the holy letter that you answer too late, because now I see clearly in the light of the end that I love you too.

AUTHOR'S NOTE

This book came into existence particularly because I've had the fortune to keep company with excellent storytellers. It would take too long to identify all of the wellsprings of narrative that I've incorporated, yet I have to mention Steinólfur Lárusson of Fagradalur, Gunnsteinn Gíslason of Norðurfjörður, Guðjón Guðmundsson of Bakkagerði on Selströnd (d. 2010), and his son Guðmundur Heiðar (d. 2009). My hope is that I've managed to convey a fraction of the storytelling spirit of these men, whereas all of the distortions and changes that their material has undergone in this book are my responsibility. The verse "If of himself the advisor took measure" is by Kristján Samsonarson of Bugðustaðir (d. 2004). I wrote the verse as I learned it, a bit differently than is recorded in the collection of verses published online by the District Archive for Skagafjörður. The poem "Life is reverie and dream" I wrote as I learned it from my grandmother, Vilhelmína Pálína Sæmundsdóttir (d. 2003). She had learned it from her mother, Kristín Sigríður Jónsdóttir of Kambur in Árnes Parish (d. 1978), and everything suggests that Kristín learned it from her mother, Vilhelmína Pálína

Guðmundsdóttir of Kjós in Árnes Parish (d. 1900). Whether she learned the poem from her mother, Guðríður Jónsdóttir (d. 1898), or from someone else, is impossible to know, but there were always many visitors and much poetry in Kjós, which lay on the main route over Trékyllisheiði Heath. In a recent obituary, the poem was attributed to the poet Páll Ólafsson (d. 1905). That's doubtful, and the poem isn't to be found in editions of his collected works. I prefer to view the piece as a popular poem until evidence to the contrary is uncovered.

BB

GLOSSARY

Reply to a Letter from Helga includes many references to classic Icelandic texts. To assist the reader in tracing these allusions to their source, the author and translator have compiled a chapter-by-chapter glossary. We hope you enjoy discovering these texts that are so central to Icelandic literature, which can be found in English translation in the Penguin Classic *The Sagas of the Icelanders*, Viðar Hreinsson's *Complete Sagas of the Icelanders*, and online through the *Online Medieval and Classical Library*.

Chapter 1: Hallgrímur Pétursson: An Icelandic poet who lived from 1614 to 1674. He is particularly renowned for his *Passion Hymns*, a collection of hymns to be sung during Lent, as well as for the Icelandic funeral hymn, "Allt eins og blómstrið eina" ("All as the One Blossom," also known as "On Death's Uncertain Hour"). "Welcome to it, when it comes," is from this hymn.

Chapter 2: Hallgerður: Hallgerður Langbrók is one of the Icelandic sagas' most memorable characters, known for her stubbornness and inability to forgive. As told in *Njáls saga*, when her husband is on the verge of being killed by his enemies, he asks her for a lock of hair with which he can make a new bowstring and continue the fight, but she refuses, saying, "Do you remember the time that you slapped me?"

Chapter 3: *Sturlunga saga*: A thirteenth-century compilation of accounts of contemporary events in Iceland, written by Sturla Þórðarson (1214–1284). In the *Íslendinga saga* (*Saga of the Icelanders*), a part of *Sturlunga saga*, the chieftain Gissur Þorvaldsson hides in a whey tub during an attack on his farm at Flugumýri, following the wedding of his son Hallur. In this dramatic scene the attackers thrust spears into the tub as Gissur, in the cold whey, shields his belly with his hands—yet he does not shake and thereby give himself away. (The attackers by this point have set the farm on fire.)

Hávamál (*Sayings of the High One*): A poem in the *Poetic Edda*, a collection of Old Norse mythological and heroic poems preserved in the thirteenth-century manuscript *Codex Regius*. "Sorrow devours the heart" is from stanza 121.

Chapter 4: The ogress Gjálp in *Snorra Edda*: According to the *Skáldskaparmál* (*Language of Poetry*) a treatise on skaldic poetry contained in Snorri Sturluson's (1179–1241) *Snorra Edda* (known in English as *Snorri's Edda*, the *Prose Edda*, or the *Younger Edda*), Gjálp is a giantess who stands astride the river Vimur and urinates into it, causing it to rise so much that the current reaches to the shoulders of the god Þórr, who crosses the river on his journey to the dwelling of the giant Geirröðr, Gjálp's father.

Chapter 5: "This green patch was like ivory in oak, as was said of Þórr when he came among other men": This description of the god Þórr is found in the *Prologue* to Snorri Sturluson's *Prose Edda* (see the note to Chapter 4).

"Bleeding is the heart that begs": From *Hávamál*, stanza 37 (see the description under Chapter 3, above).

Katla in *Eyrbyggja saga*: In the medieval Icelandic *Eyrbyggja saga* (*The Saga of the Ere-Dwellers*) (chapter 20), the temple priest Arnkell and his companions come to the farm of Katla, a woman skilled in witchcraft, in order to take vengeance for Katla's son Oddur having cut off the hand of Auður, the wife of Þórarinn the Black. Katla uses magic to hide Oddur, after which the group leaves. They return three times before Katla finally says, "You're becoming quite regular callers." Finally they kill Oddur and later stone Katla to death. See Hermann Pálsson and Paul Edwards, translators, *Eyrbyggja saga* (London: Penguin, 1989), 62.

Chapter 6: "When the call comes, no one buys his way out": From Hymn 273, "All as the One Blossom," by Hallgrímur Pétursson (see the note under Chapter 1, above).

"Day gave men barely any precious light": From the poem "Eikarlundurinn" ("The Oak Grove") by Páll Jónsson (1530/34–1598).

Chapter 7: "The road to Steinastaðir wasn't long": This is from the refrain to a medieval Icelandic dance tune/song about Gaukur Trandilsson, a figure from the tenth century who supposedly lived at the farm Stöng in Þjórsárdalur (southwest Iceland).

Chapter 8: *Skugga-Sveinn*: The title of a play written by the Icelandic poet Matthías Jochumsson (1835–1920), and originally titled *Útilegumennirnir* (*The Outlaws*).

Sigurður Breiðfjörð: Icelandic poet who lived from 1798 to 1846. These verses are from his ballad collection *Númarímur*. *Grettis saga*: In the medieval Icelandic *Grettis saga* (chapter 18), the eponymous hero, the outlaw Grettir, fights with and chops off the head of a mound dweller named Kar and takes his treasure; Grettir then declares that "many a small thing happens late in the evening" as he enters the hall of Þórfinnur (Kar's son) with the treasure.

Chapter 9: "Up onto the keel": The thirteenth-century Icelandic warrior Þorir Jökull Steinfinnsson is said to have recited a poem before his execution after the battle of Örlyggsstaðir, fought on August 21, 1238, in Skagafjörður in north Iceland. The first lines of the poem are *Upp skal á kjöl klífa/ köld er sjávar drífa* ("Up onto the keel you climb, cold is the sea brine").

Guillemot: The name of a novel (in Icelandic, *Svartfugl*), by Gunnar Gunnarsson (1889–1975). The novel is based on a famous case of homicide in Iceland, when, in 1802, a man named Bjarni Bjarnason (Bjarni's "namesake") and a woman named Steinunn Sveinsdóttir, who were having an affair, murdered their respective spouses at the farm Sjöundá in the Westfjords.

Chapter 10: Gunnar from Hlíðarendi: A hero of the medieval Icelandic *Njáls saga*. The saga says that when he strikes at his opponent Vandill during a river battle, three blades can be seen in the air at once (chapter 30).

"The first to light the fires seldom enjoy their warmth": From the poem "Konan sem kyndir ofninn minn" ("The Woman who Lights my Stove"), by the poet Davíð Stéfánsson (1895–1964).

Passion Hymns: See the note on Hallgrímur Pétursson (under Chapter 1 above).

Vídalín's Sermons: A collection of sermons for home reading, written by Jón Þorkelsson Vídalín (1666–1720), scholar, preacher, Latin poet, and bishop of Skálholt. These sermons are among the most popular literature in Iceland, even to this day.

Chapter 11: "Guðrún's cheeks turned scarlet and she married Bolli out of sheer pride": A reference to Guðrún Ósvífardóttir, a character in the medieval Icelandic *Laxdæla saga*. Her cheeks turn bloodred as she listens to her dreams being interpreted (chapter 33), and she marries Bolli Bollason because of a false rumor that the man she loves, Kjartan, is engaged to Ingibjörg, the sister of King Óláfur Tryggvason (chapter 42).

"Woman is sometimes my grief": Björn the Champion of Breiðavík, a character in *Eyrbyggja saga*, declares this in a poem lamenting past pleasures and the dying of the day (chapter 29).

"A bright and pure maiden loves me": From the poem "Meyjarmissir" ("Missing a Maiden"), by Stefán Ólafsson (1619–1688).

"Souls who love will never be parted": From the poem "Ferðalok" ("Journey's End"), by Jónas Hallgrímsson (1807–1845). The original line (in translation) reads: "Not even eternity can part souls that are sealed in love."

Chapter 12: "Curse this hag, I say, as Grettir said of the old woman": From the medieval Icelandic *Grettis saga* (chapter 78). The old woman Þuríður is known for her witchcraft and magic, and comes with her foster son Þorbjörn Öngull out to Drangey Island to attack the outlawed hero Grettir. She lays a curse on Grettir, and when he hears it he exclaims "Curse that hag!" Later she sends a log with a spell on it out to Drangey, and when Grettir attempts to cut it, his ax glances off and cuts his leg (mimicking her thigh injury after Grettir threw a stone into the boat and broke it). Grettir's wound festers and weakens him so much that his enemies are finally able to kill him.

Chapter 13: Skallagrímur: Skallagrímur Kveldúlfsson, the father of the renowned tenth-century Viking and poet Egill Skallagrímsson, was, according to the medieval *Egils saga* (chapters 1 and 30), a skilled carpenter and great ironsmith.

Chapter 14: "...the good that I will, I do not; but the evil that I hate, I do...": see Paul's letter to the Romans, chapter 7, verses 15 and 19.

"With age comes cowardice": From the medieval Icelandic *Hrafnkels saga Freysgoða* (*The Saga of Hrafnkel the Priest of Freyr*) (chapter 17), when a woman eggs on Hrafnkell about avenging murders.

Chapter 17: "I thought like Garún in the story": A reference to the popular Icelandic ghost story "The Deacon of Myrká." In the story, a woman named Guðrún expects a visit from a deacon who is to accompany her to a Christmas feast, but the deacon drowns on his way to her. Eventually a knock comes at the door, but when another woman opens the door and no one is there, Guðrún says that it must be for her. "Garún" is the form of the name used by the ghost of the deacon, since it cannot pronounce "Guð" (the word for God), which is the first part of Guðrún's name.

ABOUT THE AUTHOR

Sigfús Már Pétursson, 2009

Bergsveinn Birgisson holds a doctorate in Norse philology and has an expansive background in folklore, oral histories, and lyrical poetry. A true academic at heart, Birgisson has spent his life studying language and how it represents the truth of the human condition. He currently resides in Bergen, Norway, where he continues to write classical tales of love and masters new languages. *Reply to a Letter from Helga* is Birgisson's third novel, and his first to be translated into English.

ABOUT THE TRANSLATOR

 Philip Roughton is an award-winning translator of modern Icelandic literature and a scholar of Old Norse and medieval literature. He holds a PhD in comparative literature from the University of Colorado, Boulder, and has taught literature there and at the University of Iceland. His translations include novels by the Nobel Prize–winning author Halldór Laxness, among others. He currently resides in Reykjavík, Iceland.